PATSY KELLY
INVESTIGATES

Accidental Death

"What on earth's happened?" I said.

My mum spoke: "The maid found his body only moments ago. It seems Billy Rogers was in there with him."

"I don't understand." I looked at the impassive face of the PC on guard at the door. A scratchy message came across on his radio:

"Central calling Delta-one-nine. Is suspect still at scene of crime? Do you need assistance to bring him in? Over."

"Delta-one-nine. No assistance required. Suspect calm. Over."

Suspect, suspect, suspect. The penny was finally dropping. Billy standing to attention up against the wall. *He* was their suspect.

He had *killed* Christopher Dean?

I almost laughed out loud except that I knew it was no joke.

POINT CRIME

PATSY KELLY INVESTIGATES

Accidental Death

Anne Cassidy

SCHOLASTIC

Scholastic Children's Books
Commonwealth House, 1–19 New Oxford Street,
London WC1A 1NU, UK
a division of Scholastic Ltd
London ~ New York ~ Toronto ~ Sydney ~ Auckland

First published by Scholastic Ltd, 1996

Copyright © Anne Cassidy, 1996

ISBN 0 590 13417 5

Typeset by TW Typesetting, Midsomer Norton, Avon

Printed by Cox & Wyman Ltd, Reading, Berks.

10 9 8 7 6 5 4 3 2 1

Contents

1
In Memoriam

On the day that Christopher Dean was released from prison, me, my mum and Billy Rogers were at the cemetery. It was the third anniversary of Billy's parents' death and we were there tending the grave.

None of us mentioned Christopher Dean or his release from prison.

The cemetery was unusually full, dozens of people walking along the pathways, stepping gingerly on to the grass sections between graves, speaking in low tones. Some were dressed in black but most wore summer colours, pinks and yellows and greens. One or two giggles floated uncomfortably along on the slight breeze that moved the heavy summer air around.

It had the feel of a garden centre, not a place where dead people were buried. Maybe that was a good thing. I looked at Billy who was on his knees arranging an expensive bunch of flowers into a terracotta vase. When he finished, he placed it in the long shadow that was thrown by his parents' gravestone.

James and Millicent Rogers
May they rest in peace.

"Three years," he said in a light, throw-away tone, as if it didn't mean much to him. I thought about the boy who was coming out of prison that day. He had only served three years. It didn't seem right.

My mum was standing beside me holding a pot plant that was in furious bloom. She nudged me and whispered, "He seems much better these days."

I nodded. At the funeral, three years before, he'd been distraught, confused, unable to believe what had happened. There'd been dozens of people, all in black then, even though the sun had been shining gloriously. There'd been Billy's parents' friends from work; neighbours from the street; friends from the local clubs they'd been involved in. As well as that there'd been teachers and pupils from school.

Ever since then it had just been the three of us. Each anniversary, fresh flowers and plants, a moment's thought about the dead people. It wasn't much to ask.

I looked closely at Billy as he gazed at the marble headstone, polished up to look like glass. He was completely relaxed, as if being there was a natural thing for him. He even seemed to be mouthing the words of a song, his shoulders lifting rhythmically to some silent beat. His hands were resting loosely on his hips. I noticed his arms and face looked tanned and his hair had been bleached by the sun. He was an attractive-looking young man but then I had always known that.

"Shall we go?" he said, a smile on his face.

I was suddenly glad that I'd come. It hadn't been the depressing affair that I'd thought it would be. The three of us linked arms and walked among the laid-out graves that looked, in the distance, like hundreds of beds with fancy headboards; a huge dormitory for the dead.

I didn't know whether that was a comforting thought or not.

As we neared the cemetery gates my mum was telling Billy about the new job that she'd just got.

"It's a promotion. Still in the same college, but more responsibility."

"I don't know how you stand teaching," Billy said.

"It's not like school. Most of the people I teach are adults."

They talked on for a few minutes, Billy sounding

more polite than interested as my mum rambled on about syllabuses and classroom organization. Normally, I would have made fun of her because of this but lately she'd had a hard time. She'd recently broken up with a man she'd been involved with for a while. Ever since then she'd been packed full of nervous energy. She'd submerged herself into her work and finally got a promotion. I nodded now and then to show I was taking part in the conversation but all the while I was actually thinking about the boy who had killed Billy's parents three years before.

Christopher Dean, a fifteen-year-old boy from a well-off family. At three o'clock on a Sunday morning he had got into his mother's BMW and driven it at seventy miles an hour along a stretch of dual carriageway. There'd been almost nothing on the road when he'd crossed the central reservation and had smashed head on into Billy's parents' car. It had taken six hours to cut his dad and mum out of the wreckage; six hours with the lights of the patrol cars and the fire engines flashing frantically, the paramedics and the police shouting into two-way radios and the blades of a helicopter slicing dangerously through the dark night air.

The boy, Christopher Dean, had sustained some broken ribs and facial scarring.

He'd been arrested by the police and charged with manslaughter. His family had had the best lawyers that money could buy, though, and they'd pleaded mitigating circumstances. The boy's own father had been killed years before in a road accident and he had undergone psychiatric treatment for a number of years. He had lost his memory of the days and weeks leading up to the accident. He had been severely traumatized by it. Prison, they argued, would be the worst place for him.

Billy, who had been just a year older than Christopher Dean, had been strangely quiet throughout the trial. He'd spent a lot of his time looking at the thin, pale boy in the dock, his face vivid and red from the ugly scarring. When the sentence had been read out I had felt his hand grip my arm with ferocity.

Christopher Dean was sentenced to three years in a place called Sheldon House, a secure institution where there would be strong psychiatric support.

The barristers all seemed happy with the result. The policeman who had been in charge of the case had shrugged his shoulders and told us that it was the most we could have hoped for. The Dean boy, he'd said, seemed completely off his rocker to him.

Billy had felt defeated, though. I could tell by the angle of his shoulders, the deep breaths he kept taking as we walked out of the courtroom into the grey streets.

And now Christopher Dean was being released. He had served his time. I wondered what Billy thought about it.

We dropped my mum off at her college. I watched as she bounced off up the path, her bag full of files. I wondered if she was looking a bit too thin. I shrugged my shoulders. Sometimes our relationship seemed upside-down, with me being anxious and concerned about her. Lately she seemed like a frenetic teenager who couldn't relax and didn't seem to be eating enough.

I noticed that we were driving towards the river.

"Fancy a walk?" Billy said, parking the car.

The River Lea was full of kids on school holidays, some fishing, some just larking about along the banks. There were boys on mountain bikes and some on roller blades. We had to stand back once or twice to avoid having our toes run over.

We didn't say much for a while but that was usual for me and Billy. Most people who knew us said we were like an old married couple.

We'd been friends throughout school and when Billy's parents had been killed we'd become really close. Most of the time it was just a friendship, although now and then it seemed to be on the point of developing into something more. I'd spent a number of nights thinking about the hurried kisses we had had, the hugging and holding. The light of day had usually brought us to our senses and we'd avoided the subject, tried to forget about the passion, carried on as though we were brother and sister.

We'd been through a lot together, particularly in the last year. I'd been working for my uncle's private detective agency and had been drawn into investigating some nasty murders. Billy had always been there for me, although at times he'd been more like an annoying parent than a friend. Once or twice I'd been in real danger; somehow, though, it had usually turned out right in the end.

"How long till you pack up at your uncle's?" he said.

"Six weeks," I said. In six weeks' time I was finishing my job as office clerk and getting ready for my transformation into university student.

"Any cases?"

"Just a few odds and ends, mostly paperwork. Oh, and Tony wants me to look into the feasibility of a computer!"

"Computer? Are we talking about your *uncle Tony?*" Billy laughed.

"I know, I know. I never though he'd get one but he suddenly came in a couple of days ago with a lot of leaflets and asked me to find out about it." I smiled. My uncle was well known for being a complete stranger to modern technology. I'd suggested a computer a number of times and he'd ignored it. Now, suddenly, he was interested in one. *You have to move with the times, Patricia*, he'd said to me as though I was trying to argue him out of it.

"What about you?" I said.

"I've got my eye on an old Jag. I'm thinking of buying it and doing it up."

"Great," I said. Billy was happiest when he was working on inanimate things, engines, bodywork, electrics. He took great pride in the cars he did up, then he usually sold them without a second thought.

"My dad always wanted a Jag. Never had the money, though…"

I didn't reply. It was the first time, in three years, that Billy had mentioned his mum or dad in any context other than their death.

"I might even keep it. What do you think?" he said.

"I think it's a great idea," I said and linked his arm.

It was good to hear him so relaxed, so lacking in bitterness. Maybe he was getting over it all. I opened my mouth because I wanted to say something about Christopher Dean's release. Nothing came out though and there was an uneasy silence for a moment.

"It's OK, Pat. I know he's getting out today. He had to come out sometime. I knew he wasn't going to stay in there for ever."

"It doesn't seem right, though," I said.

"It's OK," Billy said, putting a brotherly arm around my shoulder. "The fact of the matter is he's paid his price."

The fact of the matter was an expression that Billy had started to use recently. It was his sensible side, his grown-up outlook on the world. How often I had wished that he would loosen up, act like a nineteen-year-old instead of someone who had always been forty-five.

We walked back to the car, both of us quietly thinking our own thoughts.

Christopher Dean. It was true. He had to come out sometime.

2
A Visitor

The next day I went round to Billy's on my way home. I'd rung him from work and arranged a driving lesson. It was an excuse, really. Billy lived on his own and I wanted to make sure he was all right.

His garage doors were open so I didn't bother knocking. I walked through his workshop, strangely quiet and deserted, his tools scattered about, a car up on ramps as though he'd been in the middle of something. I found him in the kitchen sitting at the table.

"Hi," I said. "It looks like the *Marie Celeste* out there."

"Um," he said, a distracted look on his face.

"Hello, Patsy," I said. "What sort of a day have you had? Oh, fine..."

"Sorry." He shook his head. "I was just thinking."

"Now, you know that's bad for you," I said, deliberately making my voice sound like a mum looking after a distressed child. I put my fingers in his hair and ruffled it.

"I had a visit today, from a young lady."

"Young lady?" I said, bemused at the old-fashioned phrase. I sat down across the table from him.

"She says she's Christopher Dean's twin sister. Sarah."

"I didn't know he had a twin."

"I didn't either. I don't remember seeing her during the trial."

"What did she want?" I said, suspiciously.

"She wants me to go and see him. Christopher, her brother."

"What for?"

"To meet. I don't know. To meet face to face."

"But why?"

"So that he can begin to make amends. That's what she said."

I didn't say anything for a minute. I was taking it all in, the new turn of events. The curiously detached mood Billy seemed to be in.

"And?"

"Naturally, I don't want to go. The last person I want to see is Christopher Dean. His sister is very keen, though. She said that there were some things that were not explained at the time of the trial. About her brother's state of mind."

"Like what?" I said it crossly. It seemed to me that an awful lot was said about his state of mind at the trial. I tried to picture this girl, this *Sarah Dean*.

Billy didn't answer. He was looking into the middle distance. He seemed to be concentrating on something. Then he looked back at me.

"It's probably a load of old nonsense. This pampered boy, who caused my mum and dad's death, wants me to go and tell him it's all right."

He got up and collected a set of car keys from the hook on the wall. I noticed he had said *caused my mum and dad's death*. In the past he had always referred to Christopher Dean as the boy who had *killed* his parents. When his rage had been at its height, during the trial, he had described him as a *murderer*.

"Want that driving lesson?" he said, in a jaunty voice, breaking into my thoughts.

"Yes, sure," I said, uneasily. There was more to say on it, I was sure.

We drove around the town centre, Billy telling me to turn right, turn left, take this fork, slow down, speed up. The rush-hour traffic was easing off and we managed to avoid any jams.

I'd been having driving lessons on and off for about a year. I was good enough, I was sure, to take my test. I'd never bothered to put in for it though.

The truth was I quite liked the lessons and the fact that Billy was willing to drive me around. And there was always the *slight* possibility that I might fail.

I came to a corner and braked too late. The bonnet of the car was jutting out over the white line. I expected Billy to tell me off about it but when I looked round at him he was staring out of the passenger window, miles away.

"You know," he said, after a few more minutes, "Christopher Dean's sister said something interesting. She said that it could be a *healing* experience for me to go and see her brother. *Healing* … like as if I were *sick* or something." Billy shook his head from side to side while I negotiated round a broken-down lorry and pulled up sharply for a group of kids who had run out into the road.

I didn't say anything, just drove on. I privately agreed with these sentiments, although I was beginning to feel mildly resentful of this female who had turned up at Billy's house on one afternoon and seemingly talked to him about subjects that I had tiptoed around for the past three years.

We came to some side streets and I positioned the car to reverse around the corner.

"Slowly does it," Billy said, as I edged back, keeping the car as straight as I could. Round the bend I turned the wheel gradually, not allowing the car to veer away, out into the middle of the road. Biting my lip with concentration I straightened up, braked gently, disengaged the gears and put the handbrake on.

"How's that!" I said, pleased with myself.

"Fine," Billy said, dismissively, and then carried on as though we'd been in the middle of a conversation. "Surely it's not *me* who's sick, it's her brother."

I folded my arms with resignation.

There was clearly a lot more to be said on this matter.

On my way back to Billy's I decided to give him my tuppenceworth. Not that I'd been asked for my opinion; it seems that the twin, Sarah, had covered all that was needed. But Billy and I had been friends a long time and he'd never backed off from giving me advice, sometimes stuff I didn't want to hear. I felt I had a right to say something.

After parking the car I said, "Why don't you go and see this Christopher Dean? It's been three years. His sister is right. Maybe it's time to start thinking about healing things."

"Like me forgiving him?" Billy's voice had an edge to it.

"No, not exactly."

Billy opened the car door and got out. I followed him.

"Well, what exactly?"

"It might be good for you. To see that he's not some sort of ... monster."

"I don't think that any more! Once I did. But now I know that he was just some mucked-up, thoughtless kid who put his foot down too hard on the accelerator and lost his grasp on the steering wheel. I don't see him as an evil murderer any more."

"Then it might be a good idea to see him?" I kept on.

"Who for? Me? I don't need any healing. I'm not sick. For him? Yeah, maybe it would be good for him. But why should I make his life easier by saying it's all right? It's not all right. The fact of the matter is it'll never be all right. I'm not going to lie to him and say it is."

I watched Billy walk up to his front door.

The fact of the matter. We were back to facts.

Back at home my mum was rehanging the front-room curtains. She'd spent the afternoon washing and ironing them. That and a dozen other jobs.

"I've already eaten," she said. "I've left you something in the fridge."

I went out to the kitchen, still thinking about Sarah Dean and her twin brother. I looked in the fridge and found a plate of what looked like risotto. I put it into the microwave and clicked the timer. When it had warmed up I took a can of Diet Coke and started to eat at the kitchen table.

In one afternoon Sarah Dean had raised several of Billy's ghosts and instead of causing an almighty upset he had been calm and logical. It shouldn't have surprised me. I couldn't help feeling a bit uneasy about it, though.

I heard the phone ringing and my mum's footsteps as she dashed out to answer it. It was Billy.

"It's me. I was a bit over the top this afternoon. You got the brunt of it," he said.

"That's all right," I said.

"No, really. I've thought about what you said. And I got a call from Sarah Dean just after I got in. She seemed to think it would do me good just to see her brother, just to hear what he has to say."

I wondered how she would know what was good for Billy.

"She's a sensible girl," he said.

Sensible. Billy meant it as a compliment.

"So I said I'd go and see her brother the day after tomorrow."

"Really?" I said, fake surprise in my voice.

"A very brief visit. No more. It can't hurt. She'll be there. It seems she looks after him mostly. I was hoping you would come."

"I'm at work," I said. He hardly needed me there at all. It seemed he'd made all the arrangements with Sarah Dean. I pursed my lips.

"Just for a couple of hours, in the afternoon. Please."

"OK," I said, begrudgingly.

"I'll pick you up from Tony's about two."

I put the phone down and felt a niggle of annoyance that someone I had never met was organizing me and my friend. Underneath it, though, was a flutter of interest. Christopher Dean and his sensible sister Sarah; I wondered what it would be like to meet them.

3
In Charge

It was the Friday before my uncle Tony's annual holiday to Ireland and I was in his office getting last-minute instructions. He was sitting behind his desk combing his newly grown moustache. In front of him was a small mirror that he was looking deeply into.

"Sit down a minute, Patricia," he said, without glancing up at me. He picked up a tiny pair of scissors and began to snip at bits of the moustache.

"When are you leaving?" I said, hoping he wouldn't ask me how I thought he looked.

"Tomorrow morning, crack of dawn. Taking the car to the ferry then across to Dublin."

"Is Aunt Geraldine excited?" I said, my notepad in my hand.

"Frantic. She's shopping as though we're going on holiday for four months, not four weeks."

"Well, you don't have to worry about anything here," I said. "I'll keep everything ticking over while you're away."

Four weeks without my uncle Tony leaning over my shoulder. It was going to be *bliss*.

"That's what I want to talk to you about," he said, turning sideways, his eyes swivelling so that he could still see in the mirror.

I groaned inwardly and got my pen ready. He proceeded to give me a list of dos and don'ts, most of them so obvious that a five-year-old could have coped. While he was talking I nodded my head and looked from time to time at his desk. It was amazingly tidy. A leather blotter pad and matching pen stand, bought, no doubt, by my Aunt Geraldine. A couple of notepads and a file that had been stacked tidily. Some hardbacked books and, to the side, the push-button phone that connected him to my office and the outside world. No computer or fax machine, as yet.

In front of the blotter was a small handmade wooden box that I hadn't noticed before. It was filled with blue cards. The words, in italics, *ANTHONY HAMER INVESTIGATIONS INC*, were visible. Still nodding, I leant across and took a handful.

"These cards are good," I said, but he ignored it

and carried on giving me instructions. He eventually slowed down a bit and began to search for his words a bit more carefully when it came to talking about the cases I'd been involved in.

"You've had some luck in the past, Patricia. I don't want you to think that I don't appreciate the work you've done for the agency. I do. But it's dangerous to get too blasé, to think that just because you've solved a murder case it makes you…" He was searching for a word. In my head I thought of *invincible, marvellous, brilliant, unbeatable…*

"Over-confident," he said.

"No." I shook my head.

"I'm leaving you *in charge*. Don't take on any new cases. Any new clients, you take their details and tell them when I'll be back. If it's urgent, then refer them on to one of the other agencies."

I nodded my head. He was leaving me *in charge*. It was like being the leader of a gang of one. I looked at the blue cards in my hands. I wondered what it would be like to have the words, *PATSY KELLY, PRIVATE INVESTIGATOR* on them.

"All I want you to do is to look after the office side of things and to do window shopping for the computer."

I nodded, a smile playing around my lips. My uncle looked up from fiddling with his facial hair. He caught my expression and sighed heavily.

"A *serious* look, Patricia. I'll admit that I've been a

bit behind in the area of new technology. But that's all going to change!"

He opened his side drawer and got out a small bottle of aftershave.

"The onward march of technology. We can't be dinosaurs!" He dripped some of the aftershave on to his fingers and started to dab it on and around his moustache. I wondered if he'd been this vain when he was in the police force. I looked down at my notepad. Underneath the word *computer* I wrote *dinosaurs*.

"How's your mother?" he said, tidying away the mirror and the aftershave into his drawer.

"OK," I lied. The whole family had been concerned about her since she'd broken up with her last boyfriend.

"I knew he was trouble," my uncle said, sitting back in his chair. There was an aura of self-satisfaction about his relaxed posture, the way he loosely clasped his hands together. How different he was from my mum; married to the same woman for twenty-five years, two grown-up children with respectable, well-paying jobs. A nice house, nice cars; a nice life. The last thing I wanted was his opinion on how my mum should organize her love life.

As I walked towards the office door I could hear his voice, tentative. "What do you think about the moustache, Patricia? How do you think it makes me look? Be honest now."

I turned round and, keeping a straight face, said, "Different. It makes you look different."

"Yes," he said seriously. "I thought that too."

Billy picked me up at about one-thirty. When he saw me he held out a packet of Strawberry Fruitellas, my favourites.

He was driving the Jaguar. It was black with a soft-top roof. One of its doors was dented in and the paintwork across the front was damaged.

"I bought it yesterday. What do you think?"

I wasn't sure. "It's different," I said.

"It'll look better in a few weeks, trust me."

I got into the car and saw, on the passenger's seat, a piece of lavender-coloured paper. I picked it off so that I could sit down. Across the top, in small print, were the words, SARAH DEAN, WILLOW TREE HOUSE, HIGH HEATH, HAMPSTEAD.

"They live in Hampstead?" I said.

"Yes, like I told you, they come from a rich family."

Billy had recently showered. I noticed that the back of his hair was still damp. He had newly washed jeans on and a white T-shirt that made his arms and face looked tanned. There was a light fragrant smell in the car as well, aftershave or deodorant, I couldn't tell.

I looked at the lavender notepaper. It was thick, expensive. I remembered my uncle's cards and got them out of my pocket. With a pen I scribbled the words PATSY KELLY across the top of them boldly.

"Here," I said to Billy, "have a card."

"I'll treasure it," he said, jokingly, and I opened the Fruitellas and offered him one.

It took us almost an hour to get through the North London traffic. Eventually, after a couple of wrong turnings we drove alongside Hampstead Heath and stopped to ask a couple who were out walking their dog. They gave us a complicated set of directions that took us into backstreets, past ornate gates and security cameras. Even though we'd only turned off the main road for a few minutes it seemed quieter, the noise of the traffic far in the distance.

Each of the houses was detached, sitting behind carefully planned front gardens, full of blooms and foliage. There were no numbers that we could see, just expensive-looking plaques outside announcing the name of the house, *Cherry Tree House, Brook End, Magnolia Cottage*. After a curve in the road we could see a sign that said, *Willow Tree House*.

"Here we are," I said. Billy didn't say anything. The car pulled quietly up to the kerb and he took a few seconds putting it into neutral, pulling the handbrake on, turning the key and pulling it from the ignition.

The Deans' house was three storeys high,

designed to look like an overgrown cottage. It had a thatched roof and leaded windows; Virginia creeper covered a lot of the brickwork. It was surrounded by a low wall, with an ornate iron gate at the side. By the house was a willow tree, almost white-green in colour, its foliage hanging and resting on the ground.

"I don't know if I can go in," Billy said, tapping his fingers lightly on the steering wheel.

"Oh, come on! We've come all this way."

"I don't know if I'll be able to speak to him, to be polite. I might blow up, explode. I don't know."

"It's all right, Billy. You'll be fine. You'll probably end up feeling sorry for him."

"I don't want that either. I don't know why I've come!" Billy said it with frustration.

"We'll just go in for a short time, a brief visit. You can say hello, hear what he has to say and then you can say goodbye."

"You make it sound easy."

"It is, it's simple. Then it will be out of your system."

"OK, boss," he said and smiled at me. I put my hand on his and gave it a squeeze.

"That's right," I said, remembering Tony's words. "Trust me. I'm in charge."

4
The Rich

A young woman in a dark skirt and blouse answered the door and showed us into the house. She said, "If you could just wait here for a few seconds, Miss Dean and her brother will see you shortly."

We were seated on a leather sofa in a hallway that was wider than my living room. At the far end was a staircase that led up to a huge leaded window. It made the place seem churchlike and I whispered to Billy, "How rich are they?"

"I don't know," he whispered back, shrugging his shoulders.

A door opened from further down the hall and a fair-haired young woman came forward. She smiled and held out her hand. "Billy, I'm so glad you decided to come."

He shook her hand awkwardly as her eyes turned to look at me.

"You must be Patsy. I'm Sarah Dean. Thanks for coming. Billy said you work as a private detective. How interesting for you."

For some reason I wished that Billy hadn't mentioned it. I felt embarrassed, and half held my hand out but then dropped it again. Had she wanted to shake hands with me? I wasn't sure.

"My brother is in the summer house. He's in very good spirits today and looking forward to meeting both of you."

"Look," Billy said, "I don't really know how I'm going to feel…"

Sarah Dean put her hand on to Billy's arm and shushed him. It was an odd thing to watch and it made me feel like an outsider.

"No expectations, Billy. You just come and see Chris. You must leave the moment you feel uncomfortable. There are no pressures on you."

I looked at her pale hand contrasting with Billy's tanned skin. Her fingers were long and thin, and her nails were carefully manicured, rounded at the ends, their cuticles like half moons. She looked back at me and smiled. It was meant to put me at ease but I felt like a kid being reassured.

As she led us along the hallway I noted her clothes. Outwardly she was dressed casually, like any other nineteen-year-old; jeans, blouse, casual slip-on shoes. There was a difference though; her jeans were an expensive brand, the leather on her shoes soft and shiny, her blouse, light and silky, like gossamer. Around her wrist was a watch with a black face and no numbers, just two gold hands pointing into the distance. Her hair was tied back with a silk scarf and in her ears were two diamond studs. Looking around the hallway at the plush carpets and heavy brocade curtains, the paintings liberally hung and the antique furniture, I had no doubt that the stones were real.

It was a different world and I began to feel very shabby in my trousers and T-shirt. I was sorry I hadn't dressed up, maybe in a flowing skirt and light top. I should certainly have worn a hat. At the very least a hat can make any outfit appear mildly exotic.

We walked down some stairs, away from the awesome leaded window, towards some French doors that led out on to a long, winding garden. In the distance I could see the edge of a single-storey white building.

"Chris likes to spend time in the summer house. He prefers bright, open spaces," Sarah Dean said, smiling widely at Billy. I noticed that her hand was still lightly perched on his arm. She glanced back at me as if including me in her conversation. I got the impression, though, that it was very much Billy she was interested in talking to. I hurried my step so that I could keep up with them.

The summer house came into full view. It was a wooden building, painted white, like a giant con- servatory that had been built away from the house. It was an odd shape, perhaps five-sided, with big, picture windows on the front two sections and long French doors in the middle. At the sides were layers of climbing plants, ivy, clematis and honeysuckle. Its roof was tiled and seemed to come to a point in the middle, almost like that of a marquee.

"Chris is still quite weak after his time in Sheldon House," Sarah Dean said in a hushed voice. It felt as though we were going into a hospital room.

Inside, the building seemed surprisingly big and airy, like a large lounge. The paintwork was a light pastel colour and the floor was made up of white mosaic tiles. It seemed to be filled with furniture, cane and iron trellis chairs, rugs and giant cushions that sat around the floor in little islands. In the corner, on one end of a long sofa, was Christopher Dean. He was fiddling with a lamp that was on a small table beside him. It was a brass statue of a woman holding a green light in the palm of her hand.

"Chris, I've brought Billy Rogers to see you. This is his friend Pat."

The young man pushed the lamp away from him and looked up at us. I was immediately struck by his likeness to Sarah Dean. In the chair he looked thinner and smaller, but his fair hair, long, almost down to his shoulders, and his facial features were very like those of his sister. The scarring that I had seen three years before had all but disappeared. I had a momentary memory of Billy's rage at the time of the trial when he'd said, *I hope he's scarred for life*. I wondered if, somewhere deep down inside he would be disappointed by seeing the boy's skin, healed and normal, his face, attractive, just like that of his sister.

"Please sit down," Christopher Dean said. I plonked myself on a cane chair quite close to him. I noticed that Billy took a few steps back and sat on a wooden chair near the window. Sarah stayed standing, with her arm on her brother's shoulder.

There was an uneasy silence for a few moments, Christopher looking anxiously around, from Billy to me, then to his sister. I found the silence difficult so I filled it.

"How've you been?" I said, directly to the young man in front of me.

"Good, good," he said and reached up to grab his sister's hand. She took it tenderly and then began to speak herself.

"I don't know how much you know, if anything, about our background." She was looking from Billy to me, mostly at Billy.

"Our father died in a car accident when we were twelve. He was a rich man, as you can see." She raised her hands in the air, letting go, for a moment of her brother, who looked suddenly lost. "He left everything to us, to me and Chris."

I didn't look round but I heard some shuffling, as though Billy was moving his position.

"What about your mother?" I said.

"He left her an allowance. They weren't very close, you see."

I heard some more movement from behind and I wondered what Billy was thinking.

"Our mother remarried three years after our father died. She brought her new husband and his son to live here, in our house. We allowed it, you see, Chris and I. That marriage has since ended. Our mother no longer lives here with us."

I heard Billy make a coughing sound.

"What's all this got to do with my parents' death? I thought that's what we were here to talk about," he said, nervously.

Sarah faltered for a moment and reached down to take her brother's hand again. He stared straight ahead and I noticed his eyes become glassy. He coughed, covering his mouth with his hand.

"In the months before your parents' death I was at school. There'd been some trouble at Chris's school. A boy had been bullied and it brought Chris's asthma on. He was home on extended sick leave. He was living here with our mother, her new husband and his son. It's these months that Chris wiped from his memory, as well as the accident."

"Ah, yes," Billy said, rather too chirpily, "the memory loss."

Billy had always been deeply suspicious of the boy's memory loss. *A bit too convenient*, he'd said.

"Chris lost any memory of those weeks here with his stepfather and stepbrother. As well as the evening of the accident."

"So what are you saying?" Billy said softly, as though he was purposely trying to lighten his own voice.

"She's saying," Chris interrupted, coughing again, "what we're trying to say is that we think, maybe, something happened during those weeks. Something bad. To me, I mean." He looked anxiously over my shoulder at Billy.

"Let me get this right," Billy's voice came from behind me, loaded with sarcasm, "something happened to you to make you get into your mum's car and drive straight into my mum and dad?"

Christopher Dean closed his eyes and was sitting perfectly still. His sister carried on speaking as though she hadn't heard.

"During Chris's analysis, at Sheldon House, his doctors said that he only remembers portions of those days."

"Bad dreams, nightmares," Christopher Dean said.

"He's very frightened by what he remembers," Sarah said. "It seems that he was certainly un–balanced by something."

"Someone was trying to get me," Christopher Dean said. He looked shakily over at Billy and then immediately back to me.

"Who?" I said, intrigued.

"Kent," he said, without hesitation.

Sarah Dean sighed. "Chris thinks that our mother's husband, Peter Kent, or his son were trying, in some way, to frighten him. The main thing is, what we're trying to say is, Chris's state of mind was not normal. His actions on that night were not those of a normal boy."

"Where was your mother?" I said.

"For three weeks before the accident she was away on a painting trip, in France."

"So Chris was here, on his own, with his stepbrother and stepfather?"

"Yes, I was," Christopher Dean said, nodding his head.

I went quiet for a moment. I simply didn't know what to say. It sounded like the plot of a film. I turned to look at Billy but he had stood up. Christopher Dean was looking nervously at him.

"I can't stay for any more of this." Billy said it quietly, without anger. "Sarah, I'm not angry with your brother any more. Not much, anyway." He was looking away from Christopher, speaking about him as if he wasn't there. "But I can't sit and listen to a story I don't believe in. He ran into my mum and dad and I suppose he'll never forget it. That'll have to do for me. I don't want to hear any stories or excuses. That just makes a kind of mockery out of it. I'm sorry but that's it."

He turned and walked out of the summer house. I stood up to follow but Sarah Dean had already taken several paces.

"It's all right," she said. "I'll go after him."

I was nonplussed. She had a sort of authority in her voice so I let her go.

"This is my journal." I heard a voice from behind me. Christopher Dean was standing up, holding a bright red hardback book.

He was even thinner than I'd thought: his jeans looked a couple of sizes too big and his shirt collar was gaping. He coughed, placing his free hand over his mouth. With the other hand he was holding the book towards me. In spite of myself I felt sorry for him. Poor little rich boy.

"What's it for?" I said, taking the hardback book.

"It's a journal. A memory journal. David, my doctor, told me to note down things that I remember, from the time when it all happened."

I opened the book. It was full of half-written pages. Every few pages there were drawings of spiders and other insects. Tiny small creatures that seemed to run through the book as I flicked the pages forward and back. On the front and back cover were the words *Sorry Billy*, written over and over again, maybe a hundred times. It reminded me of lines given out by teachers in school. *Sorry Billy Sorry Billy Sorry Billy*.

Sarah Dean came back in just then. She was looking a bit pained.

"I think Billy's OK," she said. "He's in his car."

"Right," I said, handing the book back to Chris. "I'll be off then."

"Wait, Sarah wants to ask you something," Christopher said. He was hugging his book and coughing again. Sarah Dean put her hand on her brother's arm.

"Chris thinks that it would be a good idea to hire someone to look into what happened during those weeks when he was living here with Peter Kent and his son. Because it's a family matter I don't want to involve the police or even our own solicitors. You work as a private detective. What do you think?"

"Would you take the case on?" Christopher said, breathlessly.

"Goodness no," I said, without a moment's hesitation. "I couldn't be involved in something that was so problematic for Billy."

"Of course." Sarah was nodding vigorously.

"But apart from that my uncle who runs the agency is off on holiday for four weeks. I couldn't take such a difficult case on without his help."

Sarah Dean sat down lightly in one of the cane chairs. Her brother was still standing, holding the red book close to his chest as though someone was threatening to take it away.

"Look, I'll tell you what, my uncle will still be in the office now, this afternoon. If you ring him, I'm sure he will know someone you could deal with." I got the pile of cards from my pocket with my uncle's details on them. I was dismayed when I noticed that I'd scrawled my own name across each card: *PATSY KELLY*. I chucked a couple of cards down on the table anyway.

"Ring him, this afternoon. He'll advise you."

I left them in the summer house and made my way across the garden and through the long hallway. When I got to the car Billy had the bonnet up and was peering into the murky blackness of the car's engine.

"What's wrong?" I said.

"One of the plugs." He said it crossly, without looking at me.

I stood back for a few moments looking round. I could hear Billy huffing and puffing. Once or twice I heard what sounded like a swearword so I started to hum quietly to myself. Eventually, after what seemed like hours, he stood upright, his face red and sweaty-looking and said, "Useless heap of junk." He slammed the bonnet down so hard that it made a thunderous crashing noise.

It made me jump and startled a nearby cat. A face appeared at a window across the road. I said nothing though. The car wasn't the problem, I knew, but it wasn't going to help for me to spell it out to Billy.

He sat on a low wall, his foot tapping agitatedly on the ground. After a few seconds I put my fingers in his hair and said, "You all right?"

"Fine," he said, "never better. Let's get out of here."

Maybe I'd been wrong to encourage him to go and see Christopher Dean. Maybe three years just wasn't long enough.

All the way home I didn't say much. I left Billy to sort out his own thoughts. As we neared the East End he pushed a tape into the cassette and we listened to some music.

5
Shopping

The first couple of weeks that my uncle was on holiday went smoothly. I spent most of my time sorting through the antiquated filing system that he had, arranging, repackaging, disposing of records of cases that seemed to date back ten years or more. A couple of times I got phone calls from him reminding me to do some particularly important thing, contact someone with a message or write a letter to a solicitor or insurance company that he did a lot of business with. As the days wore on, though, the phone calls stopped and I guessed that Tony Hamer, the private detective, was finally relaxing, forgetting about his work.

I spent a bit of time with my mum, trying to cheer her up. We went shopping a few times, scouring the late summer sales for bargains, jostling with the crowds up and down Oxford Street. I bought a couple of cheap pairs of jeans and long skirts that I thought would be useful when I went to university. My mum bought herself an expensive new leather briefcase, to celebrate her promotion. She also bought several CDs that had collections of love songs on them. I shook my head in disapproval but she went ahead anyway.

In those two weeks I saw Billy about three times and we spoke on the phone regularly. He talked incessantly about the Jaguar he was working on. Every time I saw him he was covered in oil and grease, holding the parts of the Jaguar's engine up to a set of diagrams he had pinned on the wall. Beside him, on the worktop, there was usually an unfinished sandwich or a cold cup of coffee.

He spent some of his time at car auctions seeing what was available and when I phoned him late in the evening he seemed tired enough to nod off while I was speaking. All the time he never mentioned Christopher Dean and neither did I. I had some idea that he was probably doing his best to forget about the young man's existence. Indeed, as the days went by, I gradually stopped thinking about the Dean family and our visit to Hampstead.

That's why I was so surprised when I met Billy and Sarah Dean out together, arm in arm.

Billy Rogers and Christopher Dean's sister – as if they were on a *date*.

It was on the Monday of the third week that my uncle had been away and I had decided to go to Springfields, a flashy department store, and see what kind of deals they were offering on their PCs. I'd been browsing through the leaflets and glossy pamphlets that were strewn about and walking along the confusing line of monitors and keyboards, laser printers and fax machines when I'd heard a familiar voice.

"Patsy!" It was Billy.

Smiling, pleased as punch to hear his voice, I turned. My mouth was half open to say something when I saw that he was standing side by side with Sarah Dean.

"Oh, hello," I said. I was thrown for a minute. If he'd been standing beside Princess Diana I couldn't have been more surprised. I looked at Billy, then at Sarah.

"What are you doing here?" Billy said. I noticed then that he had his hand on Sarah Dean's arm. On the *skin* of her arm. He also had a beaming smile on his face, like someone who had just won some money on the lottery.

"What am I doing here? What are *you* doing here?" I threw it out jokingly, looking from one to the other. "I thought you were working on the Jag?"

I said it lightly but there was a definite reproach in my voice. It sounded like a whine.

"I've just bought this," Billy said, looking down at a bag with Springfields printed across it. "It's an answer-phone."

An answer-phone. How many times had I told Billy to get an answer-phone?

"Billy needed one," Sarah Dean said.

"He did," I said, finding it hard to get my lips up-turned in an everlasting smile. "How's Christopher?" I changed the subject.

"He's quite well," she said without hesitation. Then she changed the subject. "Are you shopping?" She seemed to be looking directly at my clothes and I felt suddenly shabby and started to play with my hair, pulling it back off my face into a ponytail and letting it drop again. I launched into a speech about my uncle's desire for a computer, rambling on about this make and that and databases and spreadsheets.

They listened politely, Sarah nodding from time to time and me wishing that I could stop talking and make some kind of dignified exit.

Sarah Dean looked amazing. She had this long, flowing dress on. It was silk or some such fabric and it had covered buttons down the front. Her hair was loose except for a thin band. She wore hardly any make-up, just a touch of lipstick. There was a single gold chain around her neck and some tiny gold hoops in her ears. Over her shoulder was a soft leather bag.

"We must go!" Billy said, eventually.

"Right," I said, relieved. "I'll get back to my shopping. I'll ring you," I added pointedly, looking at the bag with the answer-phone in it.

Billy didn't seem to notice the tone in my voice or my raised eyebrows and they walked off, in the direction of the coffee bar. I stood for a moment feeling disgruntled. I let my eyes follow them around the store. Through the crowds I could see they were standing behind the glass escalator, Billy speaking to Christopher Dean's sister, his mouth only centimetres from her ear, his hand resting on the back of her hair.

It had only been two weeks since we went to Hampstead. Two weeks since he'd slammed the bonnet of the car down in anger. I'd been too busy to see much of him. He'd been working on the car, he'd said. He'd not mentioned seeing Sarah Dean.

Where had *she* come from?

All the way back to the office I kept going over it in my mind. I had this picture in my head of Sarah Dean floating along in Springfields, out shopping with Billy Rogers. I was sure it wasn't her usual shopping centre. Harrods or Selfridges or Bond Street was more her line, I thought bitchily. I remembered her dress and her hair band. A rich girl slumming it, like Alice in a reverse Wonderland.

Somewhere inside my chest was a nagging feeling of annoyance. I had been caught off guard, looking ordinary when she had been carefully turned out. There was jealousy there, too. She was with *my* Billy. He had his hand on her arm, on the *skin* of her arm. He was looking delighted with himself as well. Was that the first time they'd been out? Why hadn't he told me? He'd been quick enough to ask me to go up to Hampstead when he wasn't sure about things.

I was nonplussed, inexplicably angry with myself.

When I got back to work I went into Tony's office and threw all the leaflets on to his desk. I sat down in the swivel chair and opened his side drawer and got the small mirror out.

What I saw was an ordinary face in brown tortoiseshell glasses. Ordinary, average, these were words that really summed me up. I was five foot six, about nine stone, mid-brown, mid-length hair that wasn't exactly curly and wasn't exactly straight. My face was pale, passable, no oil painting but I got by.

Most of the time I wore casual clothes, long printed skirts or jeans and flat shoes, slip-ons or my DMs. I especially liked silk shirts and lacy fabrics and my hats. I had this collection of headgear that would surprise most people. I had several hat boxes that my mum got for me over the years and about twenty hats in all that I'd collected; some bought, some saved from the rubbish, some picked up at jumble or car boot sales.

I could look interesting. I could look good, unusual, if I wanted. But I could never look like Sarah Dean.

It didn't matter. I knew, in my head, that it didn't matter. Looks and money were random things: it was character that counted.

I kept remembering her blonde hair and thin Alice band, though. Her smile and her soft voice. *Yes*, she'd said, *Christopher is quite well.* Quite well.

I shook my head rapidly, as if trying to eject the thoughts. I pulled the pile of leaflets towards me and attempted to tidy them up. I really needed to forget about Sarah Dean and Billy Rogers.

I began to read the information on the leaflets. Bored after only a few minutes, I decided to make a cup of tea. I went out into the kitchen and leaned back against the sink. As the kettle started to heat up I felt my muscles begin to relax, the tension in them subsiding. So what if Billy had made friends with someone. It wasn't as if he and I actually had a romance going. Not at all.

I smiled in spite of myself, thinking of the times our friendship had slipped into another gear. How we'd been sitting at a table talking quietly to each other and he had leaned across and kissed me lightly on the lips. Once or twice it had been me. In the middle of some conversation, I'd be looking at his face and feel this strong urge to touch him, to push my fingers into his thick hair and pull him towards me. Afterwards, my mouth still wet, my eyes still closed, my head reeling, I'd wonder what on earth I was going to say to him about it.

The kettle boiled and I pushed the foolish thoughts away and got the tea bags out of the cupboard. It was then that I remembered a time not so long before when Billy had started seeing a woman who had worked in a travel agent's. He hadn't said a word to me about her. I'd only found out because she'd answered the phone one day when he hadn't been in. He'd seen her a number of times, I remembered, and never said a word to me about it.

Why should he? His private life was his affair, I thought, sloshing the tea bag around the cup. If he wanted to see Sarah Dean that was his business.

After I finished drinking my tea I heard a knock on the outer office door. A tiny question mark of interest formed in my head. Only new clients knocked on the office door, most of the people that we did business with just walked straight in.

I went out of the tiny kitchen and into the room that had my desk in it. Through the outer door I could see a silhouette, someone waiting. A new case for my uncle maybe. On the way to the door I got my pad out of my desk drawer so as to make myself look busy.

"Coming," I said, patting my skirt down and breathing deeply. A new client. My uncle would be pleased.

But when I opened the door and saw who it was I felt a rush of disappointment.

"The address was on the card," he said, holding it up for me to look at. A small blue card with neat printed letters and the words, *PATSY KELLY*, scrawled across the top in my handwriting.

It was Christopher Dean.

6
Memories

I took Christopher Dean into my uncle's office where the easy chairs were. I offered him tea or coffee, but he wanted neither. All the time I was wondering what on earth he had come to see me for.

He was wearing jeans and shirt, just as he had been in his Hampstead home. On his feet were some scuffed trainers. He looked like any other kid of his age hanging about in his old clothes. He was nervous though, I could tell that. He had his journal with him and kept looking at it, turning the pages as though he was looking for a reference. From across the room I caught glimpses of some of the drawings in it. After a few moments he delved deep into the pocket of his jeans and pulled out a pack of cigarettes. With trembling fingers he put one in his mouth and lit it. I was surprised.

"I didn't think you were a smoker," I said, remembering his cough. I was drumming my fingers on my uncle's desk, my eyes screwed up behind my glasses.

"Sarah doesn't like it, not at home. My asthma, you see, she worries."

Was he going to ask me to get involved in his case? I'd already said no once. Christopher Dean was the boy who had caused Billy's parents to die, and although I didn't hate him, I didn't relish helping him.

"I haven't got a lot of time, Chris, so if you've got something to tell me…" I was brisk, looking briefly at my watch.

"I need some help, I think. I need someone to tell … Sarah and I, we're close but…"

He stopped for a minute, and then sucked on the cigarette. He looked particularly small against the big padded armchair; thin, emaciated almost. I was reminded of my mum and my worries over her eating habits. He leant heavily on one arm of the chair, his book up to his chest, looking as though he was going to cough any moment. He looked weak, insubstantial, as though he might slide down the side of the chair.

I felt sorry for him. Don't get me wrong, I had no intention of taking his case on, but this feeling of sympathy surfaced from nowhere. I sat back. I could at least listen to him. It wasn't as if I had much else to do.

"Why not start at the beginning, Chris." I said it softly.

He blew out a mouthful of smoke and seemed to pull himself together.

"Remember when you came to see us the other week, we mentioned that I'd been living on my own with my mother's new husband and Jamie."

"Jamie?" I said.

"My stepbrother. Jamie Kent. It was in the months that led up to the accident."

I saw his mouth move awkwardly around the word *accident*. Maybe it made him feel better to think of it like that.

"My doctor says that he thinks I could have blanked out the whole period because something bad had been happening to me, something connected with the accident."

I nodded my head. I'd heard all this when we were in the summer house.

"That's why he's asked me to try and reconstruct my memory."

"Reconstruct?" It was an odd word to use, like putting something back together that was broken. "I thought you'd lost your memory." I had an image of something mislaid, or left on a bus.

He sat up and seemed to muster some confidence

from somewhere.

"My doctor's explained it to me. It's not that you really *lose* your memory, you just shut it away somewhere, inside your head. There are things in it that are too awful, too painful to face up to. So you lock them away."

A large brass key and lock jumped into my head.

"The trouble is, you can't get your memories back at will. They're not like files on a computer that you can just call up. Over the last three years, while in prison, I've tried to piece it all together. But it's patchy, like having only a handful of bits of a giant jigsaw. I can see them clearly but I can't link them together."

He leant over and picked up the ashtray from Tony's desk. The cigarette was a long thin one with a gold tip. He'd only had about half of it and he stubbed the rest out.

"That's why I have this journal. I never know when some piece of the past might fall out. I write it down, in as much detail as I can. Sometimes I draw it."

"Why the insects?"

"I don't know. They're just there. Sarah said I used to be interested in them, used to collect them. That's the thing, you see. I just don't remember. Whenever I try I just get these feelings, this growing fear, this sense of darkness, of being closed in."

It sounded horrible.

"Your stepfather or his son, do you think one of them was responsible for this?"

"Maybe." He said it with a sulk in his voice as though he was expecting me to laugh.

"But why, Chris? Why would either of them want to upset you, drive you mad?" I couldn't think of a better word to use than *mad*. I saw him flinch, though, when I said it and remembered that he'd had psychiatric treatment since the death of his own father.

"Because of the money. The will."

"What do you mean?"

"My father left everything to me and Sarah except for a small allowance to my mother. If either of us died, though, our share of the property went to our mother."

"But your mother wouldn't—"

"No," he interrupted, pausing only to cough, "but her husband, Peter, he had no money."

"And his son?"

He looked agitated at this and flicked open the pack of cigarettes and took one out. "I don't know. I don't know." He coughed. "I just know that the thought of meeting Jamie again, or seeing him accidentally in the street, makes me feel sick. I've had this picture in my mind of him shouting at me, screaming at me sometimes, but I can't hear what he's saying." He shook his head. "I just know that I'd hate to see him…"

"You said something about your sister," I said, leaning back in Tony's battered leather chair.

"Sarah was away at school during those months leading up to the accident."

I noticed he said *accident* with more confidence this time. It bristled slightly with me. Perhaps Billy was right. The whole story was a convoluted way of him coming to terms with the terrible thing he'd done.

"The trouble is, over the last couple of days I've been having these flashes. It's probably being back in the house again, spending time with her. She's been so, so amazing, you see. She's stood by me over all this, she's looked after me. She's the eldest, you see, she was born first."

"Flashes?"

"Memories, like snapshots from the past. Bits of the jigsaw."

"And?"

"I have this feeling that she was there, in the house, during those weeks. I don't know why, I just see her there, on the landing, in the summer house, in the playroom. Something, a noise, a smell, will bring a picture of her into my head."

He was quiet for a minute, fumbling with his book. His hair was loose on his shoulders, his face thin. For a brief moment, I saw again his likeness to his sister Sarah, the same facial features, colouring.

"Have you asked her?" I said, stating the obvious.

"Yes, she said she was at school. I've asked her a couple of times. She's very patient. I'd hate her to get annoyed with me."

"I'm sure she wouldn't," I said, thinking that I certainly would, if he were my brother.

"If I close my eyes, I can see her there, her hair much shorter, less grown-up looking." He closed his eyes in concentration, oblivious to the fact that I was sitting across the table from him. I filled the time by creating a quick sketch in my head of a younger Sarah; blonde hair bobbed at her ears, thinner, more bony, an awkwardness about her.

"It's not just the memory," he said, breaking into my thoughts. "It seems to have triggered off all sorts of feelings about Sarah. When she came in last night I looked at her and felt afraid. I was *afraid* of her."

This was paranoid behaviour, I was sure. Christopher Dean was starting to fear his own sister. I wondered about his doctor. What would he say if he heard all this?

"I have these bad dreams."

Bad dreams. What else was Christopher going to lay at my feet?

"Somebody, some boy, dressed up in my old school uniform, screaming at me, shouting at me, following me everywhere I go. I can't seem to get rid of him—"

"You need to talk to your doctor, Chris," I said, interrupting him.

"My doctor's back at Sheldon House. I won't see my new doctor until next week. Even so I can't say anything to him about Sarah. She's my guardian. I can't tell him about this. Sarah arranges everything for me. She even got Billy Rogers to come and see me."

"Is there no one you can talk to? What about your mother?"

"No, I have no contact with her. She never came to see me in prison. Sarah and I don't speak to her," he said.

I didn't know what I could say to him. I couldn't tell whether he was genuine or simply unbalanced. The accident had been terrible for him, too. Three years in an institution had made him a nervous wreck. He needed help but I wasn't qualified to give it to him. Neither did I particularly want to.

"Look Chris, like I said, I can't take your case on myself. I simply don't have the expertise. I do have a friend in the police force. A detective inspector. I could talk to her, to see if she has any suggestions."

Even as I said all this I felt that the person Christopher Dean needed to talk to urgently was a good doctor. I made a mental note to ring Billy and ask him to speak to Sarah. That's if he was in, of course.

I collected Chris's stuff together, holding his red journal for him while he put his cigarettes away.

"Did you come by train?" I said.

"I got a taxi," he said. What else?

"There's a rank just down the High Street," I said, and he left, a cigarette hanging from the side of his mouth.

I wasn't sorry to see him go.

7
Old Friends

I felt strangely deflated after Christopher Dean
left. I kept thinking, this isn't my business, it's
not my responsibility anyway. There was just
nothing I could do for him.

The piles of computer leaflets were still on
Tony's desk. I really should have gone in and read
them, organized myself, but I didn't have the heart.
I grabbed my bag and decided to go for lunch.

I walked aimlessly in the opposite direction to the
shopping centre and after a while found myself at
Walthamstow market. I bought a giant hot dog,
covered in onions and ketchup, from a shop and
began to walk down past the stalls.

Walthamstow market is one of the longest in
England. It takes place in the old High Street that

runs like a ribbon from one end of the borough to the other. On market day it's packed full of stalls that sell everything from fruit and veg to designer clothes, African art to basmati rice and plantain.

As I walked along I was struck by all the different musical sounds there were. In a short distance I caught the tones of Max Bygraves and, further on, an American country and western singer. Across the way the sounds of reggae and Bhangra competed as dozens of young kids, teenagers on school holidays, stood in small groups moving rhythmically to the music. Further down, I felt myself stirring to the sound of some American soul singer who'd probably died before I'd left junior school. My shoulders and arms started to move and into my mouth came the words of a song that I hadn't heard for ages.

I felt my spirits rising. The music, the liveliness of the market was making me feel better. I began looking at the material stalls, thinking vaguely of picking up some fabric to make a skirt. I stood looking at some silks on a stall near the middle when I noticed one that looked very like the pattern of the dress that Sarah Dean had on when I'd seen her in Springfields with Billy.

"Laura Ashley seconds, darlin'," the stallholder said. He was holding the fabric out for me. "Just your colour as well," he added. He looked red in the cheeks and I could smell a strong whiff of alcohol from him. I fingered the silk and was about to pull out my purse and buy it when, inexplicably, I changed my mind. It would look like I was trying to copy her. The stallholder drew a great sigh of breath. I walked on.

Were Billy and Sarah Dean involved in a romantic attachment? I tried to visualize them standing together, holding hands, Billy's arm around Sarah's shoulder. I even composed a mental picture of them deep in a kiss.

Did I mind? I wasn't sure. Billy was free to see whoever he wanted, just as I was.

I found myself gazing into space thinking of all this, the movement and frenetic activity of the market drifting into a kind of blurred background. In a few weeks time I was going to finish my job and go off to university. Then Billy and I would be apart. I'd also be away from the problems of Christopher Dean and his sister.

Patsy Kelly at university. Away from Anthony Hamer Inc, phone messages, unpaid accounts. *Make some tea for the clients, Patricia, see if we've got any of those pink wafer biscuits and don't forget to use the china cups and saucers.* Away from my mum and her frenetic housework, her keep-fit regime, her heartache over a lost boyfriend.

Was that what I really wanted?

My train of thought seemed to disintegrate then and I focused again on the stalls and the people and saw what I thought was a familiar face among the throng. I looked again, through the army of people that seemed to be passing by and glimpsed the face again. It was familiar but I couldn't put a name to it. I sat and thought hard for a few moments and then I remembered who it was.

It was Brian Martin, a boy I'd got to know during a murder investigation just after the previous Christmas. He seemed to be working on a china stall, talking to customers, taking money, wrapping up individual plates and cups into reams of newspaper, laughing with one of the other young men on the stall.

He looked different, fuller, as if he'd put on some weight. His arms and face were tanned and his hair had grown long and was pulled back into a ponytail. He had a nylon football shirt on and I remembered he'd been a big fan of West Ham, our local team.

I found myself smiling as I remembered things about him. When I'd seen him last he'd been working in a photo-developing business that Tony used. He'd also been a good cook as well and had, as I remembered it, some of the most terrible chat-up lines I'd ever heard.

I stood up and made a snap decision to go and say hello to him. As I took steps towards his stall I got some funny butterflies in my stomach because I also remembered that he had been quite angry with me that last time we'd spoken. I walked ahead anyway, and was only feet away from him when he saw me and stopped what he was doing and smiled.

"Brian, how are you?" I stuttered out.

"Hello, Miss Private Detective. How's life?"

"Good," I said embarrassed that he should refer so quickly to my job. "When did you stop working for Photokwik?"

"A couple of months ago," he said. "Once the summer came it seemed more sensible to work outdoors."

"You're very brown," I said, looking at his arms. There were a couple of women picking up plates and looking expectantly over at him.

"That's two weeks in Marbella," he said. "Excuse me."

I watched him serve the women, his hand lightly on his forehead as though he was thinking hard about something. He looked taller than I remembered, older as well. When the women had gone, their crockery packed up into carrier bags, he came back over.

"So, what you been doing? Still solving crimes?"

There was a smidgen of bitterness in the question but I ignored it.

"I'm packing up soon. I'm going to university down near Brighton."

"That's good," he said. "Terrible football team, though."

I smiled. He really was quite easy to talk to. I made a snap decision.

"Do you fancy meeting me for a drink or something, before I go?" I asked the question with my voice full of apology, trying to imply that I was sorry for having treated him in such an offhand way the previous Christmas. It was the best I could do without actually saying sorry.

"Oh … I…" he said, about to turn me down. "It's the start of the football season. I may be busy."

It was my own fault. I deserved it. We both stood looking at each other awkwardly for a moment. Then I put my hand into my bag and pulled out one of Tony's cards. It had my name, Patsy Kelly, scribbled over it. I handed it to him.

"If you change your mind, give me a call," I said and walked off.

He'd turned me down and I should have been feeling embarrassed, bad, rejected. I didn't though. I found myself practically skipping back up the market, joining in with the snatches of songs that I recognized.

I drew the line at Max Bygraves, though.

It was five o'clock and I thought I'd better pop back to the office to make sure there were no messages. When I walked in the door I saw the answer-phone light was blinking. I thought it might be Billy so I sat myself down comfortably and pressed the play button.

"*This is for Patsy Kelly…*" It was Christopher Dean's voice. I groaned. Was I ever going to disentangle myself from this?

"*This morning, after speaking to you…*" The voice broke down here and there was a few seconds silence. I recognized a sob and felt immediately guilty about not wanting to help him. "*I had several memory flashes and my sister, my sister…*" There was another gap. I felt my shoulders tensing up. What could I do for him? "*I've remembered a lot more of what happened, about Jamie Kent. I must talk to you, now, tonight, I can't wait for the…*" He was openly crying by then and I felt myself go weak in the stomach. In spite of my annoyance I was beginning to feel terribly sorry for him. "*Please come over to the house, now, tonight. Sarah will be out.*"

The message ended and I looked at the machine with dismay.

If I knew the boy's doctor's name I could contact him, but I didn't. I rang Directory Enquiries and asked for the phone number for Sarah Dean, Willow Tree House, High Heath, Hampstead. It was time to talk to her seriously about her brother.

"I'm sorry, caller, that line is ex-directory," a snooty-sounding voice said to me and I replaced the receiver with annoyance.

I rang Billy's number in the hope that he'd tell me

what to do. After a couple of rings there was a click and Billy's voice: "*I can't come to the phone at the moment. Leave a message and I'll get back to you.*" It was like a command. I held the receiver out and gave it a furious look. His new answer-phone!

I looked around the office for some solution. I couldn't ignore Christopher's call for help. I had no choice.

I would have to go up to his house.

8
The Summer House

I made my mum give me a lift to Hampstead. She was late home from college, though, so we didn't leave until about eight. I noticed, as we pulled away from the kerb, that it was just beginning to get dark. The end of summer; only dark nights and woolly hats to look forward to.

My mum had been looking a bit low and didn't seem to have anything much to do with herself. She seemed pleased to be taking me and I noticed that she'd put some lipstick on.

On the way I told her parts of Christopher Dean's story.

"Where's his mother?" was her first comment when I'd stopped talking. We were sitting in a long traffic jam on Highgate Hill. It was taking a much longer time than I'd thought to get there.

"They don't see her now. It's all a bit mysterious."

"And you think Billy's going out with the sister?" she said.

"I just don't know. It may be just friendship."

It was funny to say *just* friendship. As though friendship was second best, that it paled beside romance. I'd had several romances in the previous few years and none had been as solid or as long-standing as my friendship with Billy. On the other hand there was a certain excitement, anticipation, that came with romance, a kind of uncertainty that made you come alive, even if it were only for a few weeks or days. It was quite unlike anything else. I looked across at my mum's profile and thought about her recent romance.

It had lasted for months it seemed and then suddenly, one day, without warning, she'd come home and said that he'd finished with her. For a few days she'd looked winded, her face strained, her mouth seemed to be drawing in breaths, as if she'd just done a ten-mile run. There'd been phone calls and visits from friends, she'd had lots of attention. It was like there'd been a *death*.

She must have been thinking about the same thing because she suddenly said, "I saw him today." We were driving along the side of Hampstead Heath and I was looking for the turning that would take us into the backstreets where the Deans lived.

"Where?" I said.

"In college. He was seeing some of his tutors."

"Did you speak to him?"

"No, he didn't see me. He…" Her voice was beginning to break. The turning I needed was just on the right and I motioned for her to turn the car into it.

"Pull over," I said, seeing a parking place. We were still some distance away from the Deans' house.

"He didn't see me," she repeated when the car had come to a halt.

We were parked outside a house that had what looked like an eight-foot-high wall around it. The words *Cherry Tree Villa* were on a brass plaque outside. A man in a hooded tracksuit was jogging slowly along the pavement. He had a big dog on a lead, a red setter I think.

"He didn't see me because he was with someone else," my mum said. I sighed as the man and the dog disappeared into the house with the high wall.

"Oh," I said. It didn't surprise me at all. I had never trusted her old boyfriend. I put my hand out to touch her arm. It seemed to trigger off a flood of silent tears and a good deal of nose sniffing and wiping.

"Oh, Mum," I said. "He's not worth it. You can do much better than him."

She nodded without speaking, her face reddening and her eyes glittering.

"The new term starts soon. There'll be lots of new people at college. You'll make new friends, you might even meet someone…"

"I don't want to." She stuttered the words out. "I'm finished with all that. I should have known better anyway. At my age."

"Now that's silly…" I said.

Just then my attention was taken by a noisy commotion further up, close to the Deans' house. Through the darkness I could see someone running across the street, shrieking loudly. I couldn't make out who it was. A woman certainly, in dark clothes, her arms in the air, her hands on her head, her mouth open and the most almighty wail coming out.

"My goodness," I said.

"What's happened?" my mum said, her voice less crackly.

"I don't know." I opened the car door and got out to take a better look. There were other people coming out of the houses around, peering through their high gates, dogs barking loudly. In the distance the woman seemed to be kneeling in the middle of the road, one or two other people coming up to her. I recognized her then. It was the Deans' maid, the woman who had let us in that day when we'd visited. I was about to step out when a police car whooshed by, inches away from me, its light blinking blue, its siren emitting a single *naah* that was quickly smothered as it braked fiercely and the police officers jumped out.

I slammed our car door and half walked, half ran up the street to where the upset was. In the distance, parked half up on the pavement was the Jaguar that Billy had been working on. I was aware that my mum was following me and I half turned to make sure she was all right. Another police car was coming up and I turned back to see Sarah Dean standing by her gate looking aghast at the maid who was by this time almost hysterical in the middle of the road.

Where was Billy? I looked around for him, a sense of panic building up inside me, my mum at my elbow saying, "*What's happening? Why are the police here? What's wrong with that woman?*" All questions that nobody was capable of answering.

The first policeman went across to the maid but the other strode purposefully past Sarah Dean and into the house.

"What's happened?" I said to Sarah, who was leaning back against the post, looking as though she might faint at any moment.

"Mum, stay with her," I said and ran into the house after the policeman.

I shouted out, "*Hey*," but there was no answer. I shouted again, "*Hello there*," but my words seemed to echo up against the stained-glass window at the other end of the hall. I ran down the stairs and out the back door. In the distance, heading for the summer house, I could see the police officer. Had there been a break-in? Was somebody hurt? Where was Billy? My head was spinning with questions.

I got to the summer house just behind him and walked in the door. The first person I saw was Billy, flat up against the far wall, his hands by his sides, looking at the policeman who was squatting down, looking at something on the floor.

I took a couple of steps forward and saw him.

Christopher Dean was lying face down on the white mosaic floor. There was a puddle of blood looking like a red balloon forming beside him. It led back to his yellow hair which was matted and darkened.

"Who are you?" the policeman said, looking angrily at me. "You can't come in here."

I stayed still, though, looking at Christopher's body, his face flat on the floor, his thin frame lying partly on one side, his legs bent slightly as though he had tried to break a fall. One of his hands seemed to be in the process of reaching up to touch the wound on the back of his head. A few feet away from him, on the shiny white floor was the brass lampstand that I had noticed on the first day I had been there. There were a couple of chips in the mosaic tiles where it must have bounced and finally came to a stop on the floor. The statuette was face down and still, just like the young man a few feet away. Around the top of it were shiny shards of green glass where the bulb had shattered. They glittered on the floor like precious stones.

The policeman was speaking into his radio. "*Delta-five-o receiving. Scene of crime officer, one dead male about twenty, deep wound to the back of his head. Suspect found at scene of crime. Assistance needed to eject members of public…*"

It went on and I hardly had time to catch the words *suspect found at scene of crime* when two officers came in behind me.

"Oi, you shouldn't be here." One of them put his hand on my arm and pulled me away. Behind them I could see Sarah Dean walking down the garden, my mum beside her, talking gently. Further up the garden was the maid, being comforted by a WPC.

"I'm a friend," I said uselessly, trying to hold my step. I was roughly pulled away, though, out of the door and down the steps. One of the PCs stood there in front of me while the other one went back into the summer house and closed the door.

"What on earth's happened?" I said to Sarah Dean when she came closer. She shrugged her shoulders.

My mum spoke: "The maid found his body only moments ago. It seems Billy Rogers was in there with him."

"I don't understand." I looked at the impassive

face of the PC on guard at the door. A scratchy message came across on his radio:

"*Central calling Delta-one-nine. Is suspect still at scene of crime? Do you need assistance to bring him in? Over.*"

"Delta-one-nine. No assistance required. Suspect calm. Over."

Suspect, suspect, suspect. The penny was finally dropping. Billy standing to attention up against the wall. *He* was their suspect.

He had *killed* Christopher Dean?

I almost laughed out loud except that I knew it was no joke.

9
Arrested

The police charged Billy Rogers with murder.
Sarah Dean's maid said she had seen him
crouching over Christopher, holding the lampstand.

I was speechless.

He was taken to Hampstead Police Station and
kept overnight in a cell. Mum and I went after him
and hung around until well past two o'clock when a
young WPC led us one by one into an interview
room and took statements. The questions were the
same for each of us: *Why were you at the house? How
do you know the deceased and his sister? What was your
relationship with the suspect William Rogers?* The
WPC, a pencil-thin woman who wrote in a careful
slanted script, stopped occasionally to puzzle over a
spelling. She made no comments whatsoever as I
gave my answers.

We asked to see Billy but they wouldn't let us. The sergeant on the front desk was very courteous. He had a half-moon smile and a droopy moustache that he kept fiddling with. Billy Rogers was being held in custody until the morning when he would be taken to the magistrate's court and proceedings started. It may be possible, the sergeant said, with a beaming smile, to see him there.

We drove home in a sort of stunned silence, both of us starting to say things and then stopping. The roads were almost empty and I noticed my mum going faster than her usual speed. I didn't say anything, I just kept thinking back to seeing Billy in the same room with Christopher Dean's dead body.

There was no question in my mind that he was innocent. I didn't even have to speak to him to know this. Considering Billy as a murderer was like imagining Father Christmas stealing toys from children. It was nonsense.

At the same time I had this cloud of worry over me. Christopher Dean had come to see me during the day. He had rung me in tears, upset, anxious, scared even. If I had contacted someone, might he still be alive?

But who could I have spoken to? I hadn't been able to get in contact with Sarah. Should I have rung the police? I remembered then about Christopher's insistence that he was afraid of his sister, Sarah. I'd mentioned this to the WPC but she'd not seemed shocked or surprised. She'd just kept writing. If I'd have confessed to the murder myself I'm sure she would have kept her handwriting uniform and stopped briefly to wonder whether there was one "g" in bludgeoned, or two.

It was quarter to three when we pulled up in front of our house. That was when I remembered the red journal. Christopher's book where he wrote about his memory flashes. Had anyone found it? Read it? Did it throw any light on anything?

I didn't know. How could I?

The car came to a stop. The wheels on the road made a harsh crunching sound and the handbrake seemed to groan as it was pulled. The street was as silent as a churchyard and the sky a deep black. In the distance an owl hooted knowingly.

I had no idea what was going to happen. I bit my lip and went into the house.

We got to the North London Magistrate's Court at about ten but it took us twenty minutes to find a parking place.

We were directed to a large seating area that looked a bit like a hospital waiting room. Almost as soon as we sat down my mum nudged me.

"Isn't that Mr Walker?" she said.

I looked across to the swing doors to see an older man with glasses looking around. He was carrying a briefcase and some files under one arm. It was Billy's parents' solicitor. The last time I'd seen him was when he'd read the will out.

"Come on," she said, and we got up.

"Mrs Kelly, how nice to see you," he said, holding his hand out. "Very bad circumstances to meet in, very bad." He shook his head and then said, "Young Patricia, how are you, dear?"

I felt a flicker of annoyance at his patronizing words. I also noted that he hadn't shaken hands with me, just my mum.

"What's happening, have you seen Billy?" I said brusquely.

He looked at me through his heavy brown glasses, one eye noticeably bigger than the other.

"Not for long, I'm afraid. William is being arraigned this morning. He'll have the charge read out to him and be asked for a plea. Criminal law is not really my field, you understand, Mrs Kelly. I have a very good colleague who will take William's case on, but for today I'm here."

"Will he get bail?" I said, rushing ahead.

"His plea will be one of not-guilty, naturally." He pushed his glasses up his nose with his thumb, the files under his arm hanging there precariously.

"But will he get out this morning?"

"The verdict will be recorded and the case adjourned for reports and collection of evidence." He was addressing all his comments to my mum.

"Will they keep him in prison?" I said, more loudly than I meant to.

His eyes turned slowly back to me and I found myself looking from one normal-sized eye to the huge magnified one and back again. He was annoyed with me although he was trying not to show it.

"Murder is a very serious charge, Patricia, my dear. In these sort of cases bail is rare. It's much more likely that he'll be kept on remand. You'll maybe get a chance to see him before he's taken away."

A voice from the Tannoy interrupted him.

"*Case number thirty-seven, Rogers, court number two.*" It sounded like an announcement of a train arriving. Mr Walker turned and headed for the swing doors.

"Come on!" my mum hissed.

On remand. On *remand*. It was a nice way of saying locked up. In prison.

The magistrate looked at Billy as though he were a criminal. Billy did look rough, dishevelled, his hair not combed, his clothes still those that he had worn the previous evening. His head was up, though, his eyes staring directly ahead at the bench, his mouth set in a straight line. He looked as if he were about to say something once or twice but the briefest of glimpses from Mr Walker stopped him.

There was a lot of mumbling going on around the bench and I noticed the magistrate yawn a couple of times and look at his watch. Then he told Billy that bail was out of the question for such a serious charge.

Billy looked for a moment as if he were going to complain, to remonstrate. He closed his mouth, though, as the magistrate banged his hammer and told the court to recess for lunch. He was led away by a PC without looking in our direction. I looked at Mr Walker. He had seen some other solicitor that he knew and was chatting to him, smiling at something he was saying, nodding his head.

I took my mum's arm and we went out.

They let us see Billy for fifteen minutes, some of which time Mr Walker was giving last-minute instructions to him, information about the solicitor who'd be working on his case. He and my mum left together, my mum giving Billy a light kiss on the cheek.

We were sitting in a long room that had a number of other remand prisoners waiting to be transported to a prison in Kent. There were tables and chairs and security men hovering around but it was nothing like the visiting rooms you see in television dramas about prison life.

"Tell me what happened," I said, getting straight to the point.

"What do you mean?" Billy said it lazily, as though he didn't have the energy.

"Last night, at the Deans'!" I said impatiently.

"What's to tell!" He threw his arms up in a dramatic gesture, like there was no point in anything.

"Billy, I need to know. How am I going to help you if you don't tell me what happened!"

"Oh, right. Miss Patsy Kelly, Private Investigator. *You're* going to get me out of this!"

I didn't say anything. For the briefest of moments I honestly thought I might burst into tears. Billy's mocking tone hit me like a slap. In any other situation I'd have told him to stuff it and left. He looked straight at me. Hurt feelings must have been written all over my face.

"I'm sorry, Pat. I just…"

"It's all right," I said stiffly.

"I heard a noise. I was in the kitchen waiting for Sarah. I heard this noise, like a high-pitched crying. Really high, you know, pitiful, in the distance somewhere. It was coming from the end of the garden. I thought somebody might be hurt, I wasn't sure. I walked down the garden and the door of the summer house was open. I saw him straight away, on the floor, blood seeping out. It was horrible."

"When did the maid come?"

"I was silly, you know, I should have called for help then, at that minute. I went in, though. I suppose I thought he might be still alive. The statue thing was on the floor. I picked it up. I was kneeling down beside him when I heard this scream. It was like it was inside my ear. I turned round and she was standing there, at the door. It must have looked as though I was coming for her next."

I put my hand across and covered his. The security guards were talking to each other, making rattling noises with keys and fixing buttons on two-way radios. There was a sense of movement as though they were about to go any minute.

"Did you see his journal? You know, that red book he was clutching…"

"Red book?" He looked puzzled. "I wasn't looking around, Patsy. I couldn't take my eyes off him."

A door opened and another guard came in. I felt a spurt of panic.

"I'll speak to Heather Warren," I said rapidly. "We'll sort it out." My words were speeding up. "I'll come and visit. You'll see, this mess'll be sorted out in no time."

"Sure," he said. His face had closed up.

"Time please, ladies and gentlemen." The security guard said it with a fake politeness, bordering on sarcasm.

"I have to go," I said, standing up. Billy stood up too and I walked round the table and hugged him tightly. His body felt tense, like his muscles were all plaited up.

I left him standing like that, a lump like a tennis ball in my throat.

When I got home the first thing I did was to ring Detective Inspector Heather Warren. She's a local police officer who I'd helped in the past and she's always been friendly to me. Of course it was the Hampstead police who were dealing with the case but I thought she might have contacts who could do her a favour if she asked.

The main thing I wanted to know about was the journal. Had it been found? Could I look at it? While the phone was ringing I was allowing other questions to form in my mind as well: had the place been checked for fingerprints? Had the area been searched? Had there been a house-to-house?

She wasn't there, though. The desk sergeant said she had a few days' leave. I tutted and rang her home but there was just her answer-phone. Maybe she had actually gone on holiday.

I left a message. It was urgent, I said, that she got in touch with me.

Then I sat down on the floor of my hallway, my knees up, my knuckles in my mouth.

Tony was on holiday, Heather was away, Billy was in prison and I had no idea what was going to happen.

10
Hampstead

It took me two days to get up enough courage to go and see Sarah Dean. After the day at the magistrate's court I tried to go on as normal, to turn up at the office, fiddle about with bits of paper, look through leaflets about computers. I tried to put Billy to the back of my mind, to think about him in a benign way, as though he was just away in hospital, not prison at all.

I rang the Hampstead police several times. I left four or five messages on Heather's phone and I even rang Ireland to speak to Tony. He was away, though, in a cottage and couldn't be reached and Heather simply wasn't around.

My mum tried to help, offered to go and see the police herself. She was harassed and busy at work though and several times I noticed red rings around her eyes. She was no use at all.

On the Friday morning I couldn't face another day of doing nothing so I got my stuff together and went up to Hampstead.

It took two trains and a twenty-minute walk to get to the house. While I was on the second train I began to have a case of bad nerves. I was on my own, going to start an investigation into a crime in which my best friend was closely involved. If I didn't get it right and find out the truth, then he would end up behind bars for a long time. The train was chugging through North London, passing through areas I had never visited, streets I didn't know. I was going to see people from a different class with servants and antiques and stained-glass windows. How was I going to find anything out?

I sat up and tried to pull myself together. I fiddled about in my bag and pulled out a handful of my uncle's new office cards which said ANTHONY HAMER INVESTIGATIONS INC. In my neatest writing I had added, *Associate, Patsy Kelly*. I'd also packed a tiny tape recorder and a camera. I don't know why. It all suggested a confidence that I didn't actually feel. How was I going to persuade Sarah Dean to help me? Would she even let me in the front door?

Just then we pulled into Gospel Oak station, the place where I had to get off. I found High Heath and turned into the road. Further up the street, outside Sarah's house I could see a police van parked and a PC standing talking into a radio beside it. He glanced at me as I walked up the path.

Sarah Dean opened the front door for me, not the maid. She was wearing jeans and a black silk shirt and her hair was tied back with a piece of black ribbon.

"Megan's still too shocked to work. I've sent her to her parents for a couple of days," she said, holding the door open for me. "Come through to the sitting room."

I let the front door shut behind me and thought, step one, *inside the house*. Step two, *getting Sarah to help me*; that was going to be harder.

The sitting room was at the back of the house; a long thin room that jutted out above the garden. We sat close to the window in two honey-coloured wooden chairs with gingham cushions. The lawn stretched away from us. At the bottom we could plainly see the white ribbon that had been hung around the summer house; the words POLICE AREA KEEP CLEAR were printed over and over again, like a loop on a cassette tape.

"I really don't know why you've come," Sarah Dean said. She had crossed her legs neatly and woven her fingers together. I noticed then that she had no make-up on, her eyes were a little puffy and her skin redder than before.

"You don't believe that Billy did this to your brother." I said it flatly.

"Why shouldn't I?" she said, avoiding looking straight at me. "Actually, I blame myself. It was me that pressured him to come and meet Chris."

"But you saw him after that. That other day, in the department store, I saw you together. You looked like a real couple," I said. There was no point in beating about the bush.

"We were friendly. I liked him. When he rang me, two, three times, I said I'd go out with him. I still kind of felt sorry for him, you know, with his parents…"

"So it wasn't a romance?" Part of me wanted her to say no.

"It might have been. It could have developed. We'd only seen each other half a dozen times."

Half a dozen times! That was certainly long enough to fall for somebody. I changed the subject.

"When I saw you a couple of weeks ago you asked me if I could take your brother's case on. If I could help you find out what had happened to him three years ago, before he ran into Billy's parents."

"It's all a bit academic now, isn't it? Chris is dead. And, as I remember, you weren't interested. You said you didn't want to get involved."

I ignored the nastiness in her voice and carried on.

"Your brother came to see me on Monday, after I saw you and Billy. He said he'd begun remembering more and more about what had happened to him. He told me that he felt *afraid* of his memories. Then he rang me, much later, in tears, and asked me to come and talk to him. I tried to get in touch with you but I couldn't. I'm sure he had remembered something important."

I'd deliberately left out the things that Christopher had said about being afraid of Sarah.

"Have you told the police this?" she said. I noticed she was looking intently at the back of her hands.

"Yes, I have. Not that they seemed too interested. The case is closed according to them."

"But he was there. *Billy* was there, with the lamp in his hand. Megan saw it. My brother was lying dead on the floor!" She looked miserable.

"Did they find his journal?" I said.

"What? The journal?"

"Did they find it?"

"I don't know! Yes, no. I'm not sure. Why are you asking?"

"Because when he rang me he said he'd remembered something. He would have written whatever it was in that book."

"So?"

"So, maybe that was why he was killed. Maybe whatever he wrote in that book was dangerous for someone."

"But that's ridiculous, how could anyone know what he wrote in that book?"

"He rang me. Maybe he rang someone else!"

I hadn't thought of it until that moment. Maybe Christopher Dean had rung someone and told that person what he had told me. That person could have come up to Hampstead.

Jamie Kent. *The thought of seeing him accidentally in the street makes me feel sick.* Jamie Kent, his stepbrother.

"Could Chris have rung Jamie Kent?" I said.

"Why on earth would he do that?" Sarah said, looking affronted.

"Is there any way you could find out?" I looked straight at her.

She seemed to be thinking hard for a moment, then she sat up.

"I don't understand what you're trying to prove here. The police are sure that Billy did it."

"Look, Sarah," I said, sitting forward, inches away from her. "The police can be wrong. You know that. You read the newspapers. Look, you saw Billy, what? Six times? I don't know what you did. He came here? You went out? Shopping? Meals? Walks? Driving in the old Jag?"

She nodded, her face thoroughly miserable.

"Did he give you any sign, even the slightest hint that he was interested in your brother?"

"No, he was polite but he avoided him."

"When you were with him, and I'm not prying here or being nosy, but when you were with Billy, was he affectionate? Tender? Did he hold your hand?"

She nodded, without saying a word. Her eyes had a faraway look in them as though she was literally looking back at herself and Billy out together.

I went on, even though I didn't want to know the answers myself.

"Did he kiss you?"

She put the back of her hand up to her mouth, holding her lips.

"Yes," she said.

I felt a sensation of gloom descend on my shoulders. Of course he'd kissed her. What had I hoped for? That he was saving himself for me?

"Sarah, I don't want to sound patronizing but you're a mature young woman. You've had other boyfriends. You know when someone's pretending, leading you on. It wasn't like that with Billy, was it?"

"No. I know he wasn't leading me on. But the police said it was a sudden thing, a momentary loss of control. Billy saw my brother that night and just lost his head!"

"I've known Billy for almost ten years. He never loses his head. He's not that kind of person. I've never known him explode, it's just not the way he does things. He's the most organized, calculating person I know. If he had wanted to kill your brother he would have planned it, done it some time when he had an alibi, probably with me. No one would ever have known. Why on earth would he kill your brother and allow himself to be discovered by the maid, what's her name…?"

"Megan," Sarah said. She put her hand up and started rubbing her neck, hard.

"If I go to the police with all this they'll just write it all down and bury it in a file. He's my friend and I know he didn't do this."

"I don't know."

"Look, Sarah. A few weeks ago you came to Billy and asked him to help you. Against his better judgement, he did. Now I'm asking you to help Billy."

"What do you want from me?" she said, wearily. For a moment I felt some sympathy for her. She'd lost her dad years before; now her brother, after spending years in an institution, was dead.

"I want you to help me. Give me access to significant people. I want you to give me the freedom I need, to search the house, to talk to relatives and Christopher's doctor. I can't do any of that, comfortably, unless I have your co-operation. Most of all I need to find that book, to know what he was afraid of."

She was shaking her head. "I don't know…"

"At the very least, ring Jamie Kent. See if he got a phone call from Chris on Monday afternoon. Just do that. If he didn't, then I'll go and I won't bother you again. I promise. Just find out if he got a phone call."

She took a deep breath and got up. "It means

ringing my mother and I don't speak to her. Just wait here. I'll do it upstairs."

I let out a sigh of relief when she left the room. Step two, *Sarah was helping me*; at least for that moment.

Had Chris remembered something important about the accident? Something that explained what had happened? Was that why he rang me? Maybe that memory included Jamie Kent and he had also tried to ring him.

I tried to imagine what might have happened. Jamie Kent got the phone call, was startled, worried, came to Hampstead to talk to Chris. He didn't want to see anyone so he went around the side, past the willow tree to the back garden and found Chris in the summer house. They argued. Jamie picked up the lamp and hit Chris. He grabbed the book and crept away. Chris lay there, maybe he regained consciousness and began to moan, to cry out even. Billy, waiting for Sarah in the kitchen, heard the cries and went out into the garden.

I heard steps coming down the stairs. Sarah came in the door, a frown on her face. For a moment my heart dropped down to my ankles. Then she spoke.

"It seems that Chris did ring Jamie Kent on Monday afternoon."

"He did!" I said. *He had. I had been right!*

"It appears that Jamie was quite upset by the phone call. At least that's what my mother said.

She's terribly dramatic, though, so you can't take what she says too seriously…"

"Where is he, this Jamie Kent? Can I talk to him? Can you give me his address?" I began to gather my things together excitedly, breathlessly.

"That's the other strange thing," Sarah said and I stopped. "He's not there. He went out after the phone call and he hasn't been back since."

It was getting better and better. Jamie Kent had disappeared. I had to stop myself from clapping my hands with pure delight.

"I don't understand it," Sarah Dean said. "I don't understand it at all."

11
Investigation

"I've rung my mother about Jamie. I've said you can have the freedom of the house, that you can talk to Chris's doctor. Why do I have to go to the police?" Sarah said it distractedly. "Why can't *you* go to the police?"

"It's much better if you go there." I said it soothingly, reassuringly. "Ask to see the detective in charge of the case. Get him to go through it all with you. The scene of crime, the inquiry so far. You're Christopher's sister. His next of kin. You have a right to know those things. I don't. It will only confuse matters if I'm there."

"I don't know."

"Please, Sarah," I said.

"What will you do?"

"I'll look round the house. Not for the book. I think that's gone. Just to get an idea of Chris. I'll also talk to the housekeeper. If she's been here a long time she might be able to tell me some things."

"What about Jamie Kent?"

"First things first. We'll talk about that when you get back."

I hadn't a clue how we were going to find Jamie Kent but I wasn't going to let that worry me. I was just clinging on to the fact that, against all the odds, Sarah Dean was helping me. After what seemed like a lifetime of thinking about it she said, "I need to get changed."

I watched her go and wondered which expensive outfit she would wear to go to the police station.

A bit later I found out. It was a dark blue suit: skirt and jacket and a crisp white blouse. In her hand she had a mobile phone and she was packing it into a big bag, the kind you use to get the shopping. Even it looked stylish though, dark canvas with leather tabs and handles. She was rattling a bunch of car keys that had a giant "S" hanging from them. That was funny. I hadn't taken her for a *driver*.

The first thing I did when she left was to walk out into the garden.

At the end of the lawn the white ribbon that surrounded the summer house swayed gently in the breeze. I was struck by the scent that hung in the air. The garden was a cascade of colour. Giant blooms were straining to be seen and smaller flowers were running along borders and falling over the edges of beds. Even the trees seemed to be vigorously throwing their branches out over the emerald green lawn. The summer house was deadly still, though, its whiteness more like grey, the ivy and clematis looking as though they were clinging on, not climbing at all.

I took a walk around the side where the giant willow divided the house off from the next one along. It was an area of about fifteen metres in width, although it didn't look big because most of it was covered by the long tendrils of the willow, which hung like a flimsy curtain. Apart from that there were giant shrubs and bushes that filled the area. It would be easy, I thought, for someone to slip through here unseen, particularly in the dimness of a long summer evening.

I was at the front of the house looking out on to the street. There were two houses opposite, *Wood Villa* and *Stone Cottage*. Further along, on the right was the house outside which my mum and I had parked on the night of the murder, *Cherry Tree Villa*.

How long ago it seemed. While my mum and I were parking our car and talking about her love life, someone had savagely struck Christopher Dean and caused him to die. Even though I hadn't liked the boy – had, in fact, good reason to dislike him – he hadn't deserved that.

I walked back round the garden and into the kitchen, and looked for Josie, the housekeeper, who Sarah had introduced me to before she left. She was a small round woman of about fifty, with a soft Irish accent.

We started at the top floor, me leading the way and Josie puffing somewhat behind me. All the time she was talking about the terrible events that had occurred, the grief Sarah must be feeling, the dreadful shock poor Megan had had. She'd worked for the Deans for about ten years, on and off, she said.

There wasn't much to see in the upper part of the house. Three bedrooms that looked identical, like a posh hotel. Guest rooms they were called, although previously they'd been for some members of the family to use. Two of them had bathrooms attached and all had huge bowls of dried flowers in them.

Christopher's bedroom was at the back of the house. It wasn't much different from the other rooms. There were no posters of pop stars or footballers and no computer screen or console. There were no clothes strewn over the backs of chairs, no stacked hi-fi system with CD boxes piled up precariously.

"We hardly had time to get to know him again," Josie said sadly as we closed the door of his room. "Over here is Megan's room. Sweet girl, what a terrible thing for her to see, and her own brother only after dying a year ago."

"Really?" I thought of Megan, screaming hysterically in the middle of the street. I'd seen a couple of dead bodies myself and each time it had been a new shock, like something you never get used to. "How did her brother die?" I said. Her bedroom was neat, just like all the other rooms.

"He was knocked down by a lorry, she said, just before she went to university."

"She doesn't work here all the time then?"

"No, she's a student. She'll be glad to get back to her studies I shouldn't wonder. Sarah's room is just over there."

Josie pointed to a room across the way.

"Right," I said. Josie walked away, starting to go down the stairs. I stopped for minute, letting my fingers linger on the door handle of Sarah Dean's room. I would have liked to have gone in and looked around but couldn't think of a good enough reason to invade her privacy. It would look funny, I thought, so I turned and followed the housekeeper as we returned to the ground floor.

We walked around the living room that I'd already seen as well as a long cold dining room and small front parlour. Then we went back down towards the kitchen, passing a door that was under the stairs.

"What's this, a cupboard?" I said.

"Lord no," Josie said. "That's the playroom. You'll be wanting to look down there. I'll just get the key."

The door opened on to a gaping blackness.

"No one's been down there for years," Josie said, "and I don't think the light on these stairs works. Watch your step now."

The light came on in the basement area and I walked down the stairs ahead of the housekeeper and was faced with a long bright room that obviously stretched under the whole house. It was the length of a classroom, only narrower. At the far end I could see a wooden hut, a bit like a garden shed, perhaps a little bigger. It was made out of pine and had a door with a small window in it. Close by was a snooker table which was covered over with a dust sheet. A collapsible table-tennis table was flat up against the wall, and along the other wall was a worktop and shelves. There were several glass tanks on the top, like those used for ornamental fish. I could hear a whirring sound like a fan or something and could feel cool air blowing down from the ceiling.

"The air conditioning still works," Josie said. "That's grand."

The wall closest to us was covered in solid, deep shelving, from ceiling to floor. These were full up with toys of various types, all mostly packed into plastic tidy boxes. They were labelled as well, in neat felt-tip: Lego, Playmobile, Train set, Meccano, Dolls. I ran my finger along some of them. They were thick with dust.

"What's that?" I said, walking across the carpeted floor, towards the small pine shed.

"The sauna. Mr Dean had it put in, years ago, before the twins were born, I believe. It was a fashion, you know, at the time."

I walked up to the door and looked in through the tiny window. Just blackness inside.

"Have you got a key?" I said. I was curious. It really was like a garden shed.

"Not here, but there is one, somewhere. It's kept locked all the time."

I looked around. It was every kid's dream to have their own playroom, to own things like this. My eye caught the glass tanks.

"Did they have fish?" I said.

"Not at all. These belonged to young Christopher, God rest his soul." She stopped for a moment and touched a crucifix that was hanging around her neck. "He used to collect things, exotic insects I believe he called them. Some very big spiders, as I recall. I didn't like them. Not one bit. His mother made him keep them down here."

I remembered the spiders that Christopher had drawn all over his book. I shivered slightly. I wasn't that fond of insects myself, especially not spiders. It was something that made Billy Rogers laugh.

Illogical, he'd said, a human being is hundreds of times bigger than a spider. What was there to be afraid of?

After a few more minutes we went back upstairs and I was about to ask Josie a bit about the family history when a sharp buzzer sounded. We both looked towards the front door to see the silhouette of a woman.

"I wonder…" Josie said, walking down the hall and opening the door.

A big woman of about forty stood there, dressed in a long flowing black dress. She had blonde hair which hung in waves past her shoulders. On the porch beside her were two giant straw bags, packed full. She was carrying a bunch of what looked like flowers but when I looked closer seemed to be herbs.

"Mrs Kent," I heard Josie's voice. "It's grand to see you. Sarah's out, I'm afraid."

"Josie, darling. Thank goodness you're still here," she said. She leant down towards the smaller woman so that Josie could give her a peck on the cheek. She gave the bunch of herbs to Josie, who smiled as though she'd just been given a bouquet.

"You're looking very well, Mrs Kent. Will you be coming in to wait?"

"Nonsense. I've put on so much weight." Mrs Kent walked boldly into the hallway, past Josie and handed me one of her straw bags.

"And now this. Poor darling Chris," she said, walking off down the hall, her black skirts flowing out behind her, Josie following, throwing questions out. *Have you come from home? Or abroad? How is your painting?* In the distance I could hear the younger woman's voice, *some Earl Grey, Josie, no milk or sugar, I'm absolutely parched.*

I looked at the bag in my hand, drew a sigh and followed them both down to the kitchen.

12
The Dean Family

I staggered into the kitchen with the straw bag.
Mrs Kent had sat herself down on one side of a
long wooden kitchen table. Josie was taking cups
and saucers out of the cupboard and laying out a tea
setting in front of her. I put the bag down carefully.

"Patsy is working with the police," Josie
said, "investigating this terrible business with
Christopher."

Mrs Kent looked round at me. "My dear, I'm so
sorry. I'd taken you for one of the staff. Do sit down
and have some tea with us."

"No, thanks all the same," I said. I leant back
against the worktop. I was wondering whether I
could manage to talk to Mrs Kent about Jamie Kent
and where he might be. It was awkward, though.

Josie obviously hadn't seen her for a while and was talking. It didn't seem right to butt in. I had to wait until the right moment.

Josie was taking a cake tin from the cupboard and prising the lid off.

"Not for me, Josie," Mrs Kent said, her hand in mid-air, as if she were prepared to physically fend off the piece of cake. "I'm on this food combination diet. Not diet exactly," she turned to me, "diets are very bad for you, my dear, very bad indeed. No, this is more of a system, a *scientific* system, for ridding the body of toxins. Did you know that you should never eat meat and potatoes together in the same meal! It's dreadful for your digestion."

I shook my head, wondering, for a moment whether this woman actually knew that her son was dead, had been murdered, a few days ago.

"Not that I eat meat at all, haven't done so for, must be fifteen years or more. Can't bear the idea of eating something that had to be struck down, deprived of a life." She was quiet for a moment and Josie looked pointedly at me. "Isn't that right, Josie. I haven't eaten meat for a long time."

"That's absolutely correct, Mrs Kent."

The front door banged and I heard Sarah Dean's voice. She was back from the police station.

"It's Sarah." Mrs Kent whispered the words and she looked apprehensively at Josie, as though she wasn't supposed to be there. Her face lost about twenty years, became round and fearful. She looked like a plump teenager who'd been caught eating ice-cream straight from the fridge. The kitchen door opened and Sarah Dean stood there, a bunch of flowers in her arms.

"These were left outside the gate, Josie…" she started to say and then saw her mother. She said nothing at first, just laid the flowers on the table.

"Sarah, my love … I came as soon as you rang…" Mrs Kent said. She got up, took a couple of tentative steps over towards her daughter. She stopped a foot or so away and seemed to hesitate for a minute as though there was a deep gully between them.

"Sarah, darling. How dreadful. Poor, poor, Chris. He was just too fragile for this world." She seemed to call the words across, her hands joined low in a kind of cradle.

Sarah Dean's face was blank. An unreadable expression.

"Why have you come, Mother?" she said, the word "Mother" dropping like lead from her mouth.

"To be with you, darling." Mrs Kent stepped across the last foot of space and encircled her daughter with a single arm. A minisecond later Sarah stepped forward out of her mother's grasp. She busied herself at the bouquet of flowers that was on the table.

It was embarrassing. I wanted to look away. The older woman spent a couple of seconds smoothing down the fabric of her dress with the discarded hand.

Finally, Sarah looked at me and said, "Patsy, I've got the information you wanted. I've written it all down, here." She took some sheets of paper from the bag she'd been carrying. "I've been in touch with Chris's doctor from Sheldon House. He can't see you until Monday." She was curt, cold. I wasn't sure if it was for me or for her mother. "Josie, put these flowers in some water, will you? And bring my mother up to the sitting room. She and I can talk there."

I picked the papers up from the table and watched as she turned and went, closing the kitchen door quietly behind her.

Mrs Kent stood still for a few seconds and then said, "She's stricken with grief, my daughter. She hides it well but she is. I know, you see. I know her better than anyone."

I nodded, not knowing what to say.

"I'll see myself up, Josie. I know the way, after all." She pulled herself up straight and swept out of the room, allowing the heavy door to bang behind her.

Josie poured the tea out anyway and I said I'd have a cup.

I drank quietly for a few moments, across the table from the housekeeper, whose eyes seemed to flicker from time to time towards the ceiling, the room above where Mrs Kent and her daughter were meeting.

"They don't get on, then," I said.

"Now there's an understatement," Josie said.

"Can you tell me about it?" I said it gently.

"She'll not let her stay. You mark my words. She'll have her bottom in the back of a black taxi before these cups are washed up and put away."

"Did they have a row?" I said. Josie seemed miles away, her mind swimming in deep waters that I knew nothing about.

"Was it over Christopher going to prison?" I spoke again after a few moments' silence. I felt like I was trying to pull in an awkward fish that was heading away from me.

Josie shrugged and tutted at the same time. I tried one last tug.

"If this case isn't resolved it'll be the police that are asking these questions, Josie, not me. It's important that I know what's happened in the family."

The words, *so that I can eliminate them from my enquiries* jumped into my head but I couldn't bring myself to say it. Some days, I really did feel like an actor playing a role, and some of the lines were old and smacked of insincerity and, at times, seemed faintly ridiculous.

She took up the bait, though.

"There was a row. But it didn't start then…" she said, screwing her face up to try and explain. "It's hard to…" She seemed lost for words.

"Start at the beginning. I've got time," I said, looking at my watch. I had all the time in the world. I took my notepad and pencil out and laid them on the table.

"Mrs Kent – Mrs Dean, then – was always good to me, you see, so I can't complain about her myself, you know, but she was a terrible self-centred woman when it came to her family. As soon as I came here I knew that they weren't an ordinary family. She had her bedroom, he had his. It was a strange way to carry on." She shrugged her shoulders.

"The marriage had broken down?"

"It had finished. They were legally separated. They just shared this house, and the children. Mr Dean, a lovely man, God rest his soul, he started seeing another woman. He was mightily in love with her. I'll tell you one thing, *she* didn't like it at all." Josie pointed upstairs. I assumed she was referring to Mrs Kent.

"She was an estate agent. Mrs Adams, Rachel, her name was. She worked for Mr Dean's company, selling the houses he had built. She had a daughter too, about the age of the twins. He was open about it, bringing her here to the house, having her meet his friends and Mrs Kent – Mrs Dean, then. The girls got on well together."

"Did he want a divorce?" I said, finding myself intrigued. My pencil lay on the table, my notepad hardly written on.

"There were plans, I believe. But the accident happened before anything was done about it."

"When Mr Dean was killed?"

"Killed outright." Josie lifted up her crucifix and held on to it. "His woman friend was in a coma for days before she died. It was just sheer luck that neither of the girls were hurt."

"The girls were involved in the accident?"

"Sarah and the daughter, Philippa, her name was. Both had a few hours in hospital but came home that evening. I remember herself, Mrs Kent, Mrs Dean then, was in a terrible state. She stayed in her room for days. Christopher and Sarah stuck together after that. After their father's funeral they were very close."

Josie stopped for a moment at some sounds from the floor above.

"And, after all, it was Mrs Dean who remarried. An out-of-work actor, Peter Kent. Penniless he was. It caused a lot of arguments between her and Sarah."

"They came to live here?" I said.

"They got married on the day after Boxing Day. They lived here until just after the accident; seven or eight months."

"What happened? In those weeks before Christopher crashed into Mr and Mrs Rogers."

"It was in the July, about the middle of July I

think, that Christopher came home from school. His asthma had come on terrible bad. There'd been some trouble, some bullying. Christopher wasn't the only one affected. He was weak, you see. I don't think he always stood up for himself. He was very unwell, for weeks. Boarding schools, awful places. I can't understand how loving parents can send their young ones off to be looked after by other people."

"And Peter Kent's son, Jamie, was here?"

"Yes. A pleasant enough young man. They got on, I think. There might have been a bit of squabbling. Peter Kent got a part in some play – a *minor* part – and Mrs Kent, she went away to France. There was just the boys and me. I didn't mind. I hardly saw them, to tell you the truth."

"Where was Sarah?"

"At school, part of the time. Then I think she was staying with some friends for a couple of weeks. She took it very badly. After the accident she blamed her mother for not being here to look after Chris. They had a dreadful argument. There were things said that a mother should never hear. Mrs Kent packed her bags and took her actor husband with her. The boy Jamie had left before that, had gone back to his mother."

A door slammed from above us and footsteps sounded along the hallway.

"They got divorced. About a year ago I heard."

"But Jamie lives with Mrs Kent. Why doesn't he

live with his parents?"

"His father is in America. His mother, I believe, lives out in the country somewhere. Perhaps he likes London."

The door burst open and Mrs Kent stood there, her face red, a large wad of tissues in her hand.

"You won't believe this, Josie. Her own mother. She's throwing her own mother out." Josie said nothing, just played with the cross in her fingers. Mrs Kent turned and looked at me. "Do you know what my daughter is doing at this very moment?"

I shook my head slowly.

"She's ringing for a taxi to take me home. *Thank you, Mother*," Mrs Kent began to mimic a high-pitched voice that wasn't anything like Sarah's, "*I shan't be needing any support*. Can you believe that? I drop everything to come and see her and she dismisses me! And at a time like this. When I've lost my only son."

She seemed to tag the last bit on. As if she'd just remembered why she'd come. She leaned dramatically back against the door and put the wad of tissues up to her nose. All at once there was the sound of the front door buzzer.

"She insists on me leaving. I can come to the funeral, *if I like*!"

Miraculously, her tears seemed to dry up and she grabbed hold of her bags and heaved them towards the stairs. I followed her out into the hallway. I was hoping to be able to speak to her but it looked like I was going to lose my chance.

"*And don't bother waiting around for any money from Chris's will, Mother.*" Mrs Kent was still attempting to mimic her daughter's voice. "*There won't be any. Chris has left everything to me!*"

She threw the last words up into the air and I looked round to see Sarah Dean at the top of the stairs, in front of the leaded window.

"Goodbye, Mother," she said, in a perfectly calm voice.

"Don't think I didn't know about your visit to the solicitors, Miss Sarah! I still have my contacts. I know that *you* forced Chris to make a new will. Now I don't get a penny from my son and everything is yours. Don't think that I don't know that, young lady."

I was looking at Sarah, trying to read her expression. *She had got Chris to make a new will leaving nothing to his mother.*

Mrs Kent said nothing but gave me a kind of knowing look as though I were a co-conspirator. Then she walked purposefully down the hall and threw open the front door. I braced myself expecting it to slam loudly but instead there was just a gentle click and I was left looking at Sarah Dean at the top of the stairs.

13
Mothers and Daughters

Sarah Dean followed me back down to the kitchen while I collected my stuff together. Josie was endlessly drying the two teacups that we had used. I picked my notepad up off the table and saw that I'd managed to scribble some information down. I had something I wanted to add to it but didn't want to do it in front of them.

Christopher Dean had made a new will leaving everything to Sarah.

"Well, Pat," she said, a nervous smile on her lips, "now you've met the indomitable Mrs Kent. I did tell you she was dramatic."

"Yes, you did," I said, my voice steady, not giving anything away.

"Josie's probably told you what a dreadful woman

she is. How she only ever thinks about herself." She looked over to Josie, who was concentrating on a teaspoon that she was polishing.

"Yes, she did," I said, leaning back against the worktop.

"It was me who looked after Chris. All his life it was me who was there for him. That woman did nothing. She did *nothing*!"

The last word sounded like a hiss. I noticed a red spot developing on each of Sarah's cheeks and for the briefest of moments her hair seemed electric, the ends of it flying away with temper. Then, in a second, she calmed down and looked straight at me.

"Do you still live with your mother, Pat?"

"Yes." I thought of my mum that morning, sorting through dozens of dusty old files full of lesson notes, her headphones on, listening to some sloppy love album, from time to time her eyes becoming glassy. On my way out she'd offered me some money *to buy yourself some lunch up at Hampstead*.

"Do you get on?"

"Yes, we do," I said. It was true. Even though she was my parent and I loved her, I also *liked* her a lot.

"That's nice for you."

There was an edge to her voice, a hardness I hadn't noticed before.

"My mother is a very selfish woman, always was. It was me who cared for Chris. I was born first you see, about thirty seconds before him. So I was his big sister."

"You looked after him." Josie said it quietly.

"I was always a bit bigger than him, a bit more mature than him—"

"Brighter than him," Josie butted in.

"Yes, I got on better at school, had more friends. You name it, I managed it better than my brother."

"He was bullied as well," Josie said.

"Yes…" Sarah hesitated. "He always had a bad time in school. And then when Dad died he blamed himself. He got more difficult after that. He had a sort of dark side."

"Why did he blame himself?" I said.

"We were going to the seaside. He was supposed to come but he got into a mood and wouldn't. I was quite friendly with Philippa, you know, and Chris felt left out. There was a row and eventually we went anyway. Chris always thought that if he'd have come, we'd have missed the accident. You know the sort of thing, if we'd been half an hour earlier the other car wouldn't have been there and so on…"

"And after the accident?"

"He got worse. More dependent on me. I looked after him as best I could."

"And your mother?"

"My *mother*? Oh, Mrs Kent was too busy looking after herself. When my brother was ill and needed her she was falling in love, getting married, going off to paint…"

"And the will?"

I threw the question in casually. It stopped her speaking.

"When our father died he split everything between me and Chris, except that our mother had an income. If anything had happened to either of us, when we were under eighteen, that money would have gone to her. After Chris's accident I asked her to leave. I didn't want her near me. I changed my own will in favour of Chris. When he came out of prison I persuaded him to change his will in favour of me. I don't deny it. I wanted to make sure that she didn't see a penny of his money. There. Now you know how hard I can be." She gave a little laugh.

I didn't comment. I wanted to be alone and think it through.

"I need to get off," I said, putting my book into my rucksack. Then, remembering something, I said, "Did you ask about Jamie Kent's disappearance?"

"Ah, yes. Not so dramatic as you first thought. It seems that Jamie often goes missing, for two or three days. Then turns up, right as rain. I'm surprised *Mrs Kent* puts up with him!"

"Why does she?" I said.

"It's her link to her ex-husband. Peter the Actor."

"He remarried then?" I said.

"Yes. A thinner, younger, woman, I believe."

I left soon after. I'd had enough of the Dean family for one day.

My mum was in the kitchen when I got home. The sound of a slow love song filled the downstairs of the house and I had to shout to make myself heard.

"That's too *loud*, Mum!"

"Sorry," she mouthed. She had pink rubber gloves on and a foamy Brillo pad in her hand. Her hair was standing on end and her top looked grubby. The oven was glittering, though.

I went into the living room and turned the volume down on the hi-fi.

"Honestly," I said, marching back into the kitchen, "what about the neighbours?"

"I forgot," she said, shrugging her shoulders.

She looked pathetic and I felt sorry for her. I went across and gave her a tight hug. Sometimes, I got so involved in things that I forgot what it was like to be young and in love.

Over the weekend I looked over and over all the stuff that Sarah had given me as well as the notes I'd taken myself.

I was patient about it all. I took my time and wrote down everything I had learned about the family and the case so far. It was important, I knew, to have good, solid, records to look back on. That much Tony had taught me.

The notes that Sarah Dean had given me had been thorough. They were on the lavender writing paper that I had seen before, her name and her address printed across the top of the page. Underneath it were the details of the scene of the crime; Christopher had been hit from behind, two, maybe three blows. He had died instantly. Something about that had niggled me but I hadn't been able to work out what it was. The weapon had been the lampstand that I had seen. Billy's fingerprints were on it, along with the maid's, the housekeeper's, Christopher's and Sarah's. Everyone, it seemed, had touched the lamp at some time or other.

Underneath, she'd written in larger letters, *no red book found*. I hadn't expected it.

I'd made my own notes, taking a fresh sheet of paper and heading it *The Dean Family*. I'd jotted down, in a list form, all the things I'd learned about them. It took up four sides of A4.

The weekend seemed to last for ever. From time to time I picked up the wad of notes and looked through them, trying to spy a way forward. On the Monday I was due to talk to the doctor at Sheldon House. Other than that I had no idea what I was going to do, how I was going to move the case on.

On the Sunday afternoon I went round to Billy's house, just to check that everything was all right. I let myself in with a key that he had given me some time before. Even though it was still summer, the place seemed cold. Each room empty and desolate. I opened the fridge to find a half-full carton of milk sitting there. There was also an unopened packet of cheese and some cans of fizzy drink. I chucked out the milk and cheese and opened one of the cans and started to drink from it.

One night, three years before, Billy's mum and dad had left that house and never returned. Maybe his mum had left a bottle of milk in the fridge that Billy had had to empty out, a piece of cheese or some favourite biscuits in a cupboard. I felt this lump beginning in my throat so I made myself busy by filling a black plastic bag with rubbish.

I walked around making sure that all the windows and the back doors were locked, then I let myself out. It would be too much, I thought, just too much if Billy came out of prison to find that he'd been burgled.

Because Billy was going to come out of prison. I was sure of that.

When I arrived home I got all the papers out again and looked carefully through them. The words SARAH DEAN SOLE BENEFICIARY kept catching my eye and I was reminded of Chris's claims that he had begun to fear his sister. *When she came in last night I looked at her and felt afraid.* With Christopher dead Sarah was now a very rich young woman.

I shook my head. It was far-fetched, too obvious.

Why one earth would Sarah get her brother to change his will and then kill him within days? Apart from that she was in the house with Billy and the maid, Megan. And she was *helping* me with the investigation.

I looked again at her sheet: *no red book*. Chris had phoned Jamie Kent on the afternoon he had been murdered. Jamie had left the house and hadn't been seen since. He often went missing for days, Mrs Kent said. It was a coincidence though and I couldn't ignore it. I wrote the words JAMIE KENT in capitals on the bottom of the sheet. What exactly had happened three years before, when Chris had run out, got into a car and driven into Billy's parents?

I turned the lavender sheet of paper over. On the back of it Sarah had written, *Appointment David Geraghy Monday 10.00* and an address in Essex. Perhaps I would find out more about Christopher's state of mind from him. Maybe he would know things that might explain the accident. If Christopher had been killed because he had remembered something then I had to find out what it was. I looked at the address in Essex again.

Essex? I slumped on to the table with dismay. How was I going to get out to Essex for ten o'clock in the morning? In the past it had always been Billy who had driven me where I wanted to go.

"Hi, love." My mum came into the kitchen. She

had her hair in a turban and her skin was shining as though she'd just given it a good scrub. She looked relaxed.

"I'll clear this mess away in a sec," I said.

"A young man phoned for you. Brian somebody," she said.

"Brian Martin?" I sat up.

"Yes, he didn't leave a message, he just said to say that he'd called."

Brian Martin had phoned me. I felt this spurt of satisfaction and a smile came on my face from nowhere.

"He didn't leave a message?" I said.

"Nope," my mum said.

A picture of Brian Martin came into my head and I didn't speak for a few moments. I remembered him on the crockery stall, laughing and chatting to the women customers. The truth was I'd felt *attracted* to him that day.

"That's really interesting," I finally said to my mum.

"Wasn't he that young man who you went out with just after last Christmas?" she said.

"Yes." My voice went flat. I had seen Brian Martin a few times. At first it had been because I'd wanted some information from him but then I began to really like him. He'd been hurt though, had accused me of treating him dishonestly.

"I thought he'd finished it?" my mum went on.

"He did. He did," I said, remembering his angry face and cutting words.

"He sounded really nice on the phone. I think it would do you good. To get out and have a nice time. What with all this business with Billy Rogers…"

I'd stopped listening to her, though. I got up excitedly and began to collect my things together. A smidgen of an idea was forming in my head. Brian Martin had a car, I remembered. Could I possibly, after the bad way I had treated him before, could I possibly ask him to drive me out to Essex to see Christopher Dean's doctor?

Was it fair to ask that of him?

Did I have the brass neck to do it?

"I'm just going upstairs to make a phone call," I said. Delight and trepidation were mixing together like a lethal cocktail inside of me.

14
The Doctor

Brian Martin came for me at about eight-thirty. I opened the front door to find him leaning against the wall of the porch.

"Hi, Patsy," he said, and some tiny thing inside my chest did a somersault. Don't ask me why. He was in jeans and a check shirt. His hair was loose on his shoulders and he had sunglasses on. When I followed him out to the car, he turned and looked straight at me and said, "You tell me where to go and what you want me to do. But, one thing, Patsy, don't tell me any lies or lead me up any dead ends. Otherwise you and me won't be friends for long."

I nodded, clutching my *British Isles Map Book*, my mum's new briefcase and a hat I'd selected to wear but suddenly didn't have the courage to put on.

I got in the car and said, "The A12 eastwards. It's a couple of miles past Brentwood."

"OK, boss," he said and we drove off.

I'd been up since six trying to decide what to wear. Not because I was seeing Brian, although that thought had been hanging around in the back of my mind. I had to meet David Geraghy, the doctor who had worked with Christopher while he was in Sheldon House. I couldn't turn up in jeans and T-shirt.

It was one of the things I'd learned in the year of working with my uncle. The way you looked mattered. Most of the job of being an investigator was based on talking to people, trying to get them to tell you things, to trust you.

The cases that usually came to a private investigations agency like my uncle's were old, unsolved crimes that the police had given up on, missing people, insurance claims, petty vandalism or shoplifting.

My uncle's job (and mine sometimes) was to meet people that the police had probably already spoken to and persuade them first that it was worth speaking to us and second that we could be trusted to treat their information as confidential.

They had to have some sort of faith in us and the only way we could gain that in the absence of a policeman's uniform or credentials was to look and sound like someone they could trust, have confidence in. This is where my age usually went against me unless it was a case involving young people. I'd had some success in these over the last year. David Geraghy was a professional man, though, a doctor. I had to look just right.

I imagined someone quite old, wearing a white coat with several pens in the top pocket. A grey-haired man in an office lined with books; a heavy oak desk and a leather couch for patients to lie down on so that he could find out what was troubling them.

I needed some conservative clothes, so I rummaged in my mum's wardrobe and came up with a roomy straight dress and a dark jacket to go over the top. I'd pulled my hair back into a tie at the back of my neck and found some button earrings.

I'd sat in front of the mirror for some time wondering whether to put on some make-up. I'd got my eye liner out and painted a thickish line on my eyelid but didn't like the effect and took it off with some lotion and cotton wool.

I like wearing make-up, don't get me wrong. I've got nothing against it in principle. What I hate, though, is the thought of painting a face on and having to wear that particular mask every day, worrying in case part of it should crack and that someone might see the real you coming through. I always remembered girls in the toilets of pubs or discos rushing to the mirrors to *repair* their make-up as though it was part of a machine that had broken down.

I like putting different colours on my face, giving

it a particular look, but I also like just washing it and going out, not having to worry about whether my lipstick stains a cup or my mascara rubs off on to my skin.

I decided, in the end, for a little bit of blusher and some pastel lipstick. I gave my glasses a good clean and then went to get all my stuff together. I looked in dismay at my rucksack. It was no good at all; black nylon with fluorescent pink sections, a couple of *Save the Whale* stickers on it and one of the outside pockets was coming off where it had caught on something. It shouted the words, *student, teenager, untrustworthy, incompetent*. Beside it, sitting suavely on the floor, was my mum's brand new, brown leather briefcase. There was just no contest.

When I left, she was still out on her run. I left her a note and offered her the use of my rucksack for the day.

It was only fair.

"Why are you so sure your friend didn't do it? It sounds pretty cut and dried to me," Brian said, after I'd given him a potted version of events.

"Because I know him so well. We're very close. It's hard to explain."

"I did get that feeling," he said, referring to the time when he and Billy and me were in a kind of triangle. I ignored it.

"Christopher Dean was sure that something had

happened to him at the time of the accident. The trouble was his mind had blanked out those weeks leading up to it. In the days after Billy and I had gone to see him, he was beginning to remember more of what had happened. When he came to see me he gave me the impression that he was afraid of Jamie Kent. Then he rings me up and says he's remembered something important. He also rings Jamie Kent, who is upset by the phone call, goes out and isn't seen again. And that night, that very night, Christopher is murdered and the journal is missing. Doesn't that seem odd to you?"

"But didn't you also say that Christopher said he was afraid of his sister?"

"Yes, I did." I sat quietly for a minute. Sarah and the New Will. It was the one bit of the puzzle that was sticking out awkwardly.

"Why not go to the police with your theory? They're not that bad, you know."

I smiled. It had gone out of my mind that Brian's dad was a police officer.

"When my inspector friend comes back off holiday, then I'll go to the police. She'll take me seriously, I'm sure. Meanwhile I'll just carry on trying to find out about Christopher's past and wait until Jamie Kent turns up."

We sat silently for a few minutes, then I noticed signs for Brentwood appearing in front of me. I picked up the map book and began to look at it.

"Take the next exit," I said, "then the second exit on the roundabout. It's about a mile or so on from that."

On the dashboard, in front of me, I noticed a purple and light blue sticker, *Follow the Hammers*.

"How are West Ham doing?" I said, out of politeness. I was more interested in nuclear physics than I was in football.

"Oh, you know, lots of injuries in the team, players sold but none bought. It doesn't look hopeful for the season. It'll be a struggle to stay up in the League." Brian shrugged his shoulders and shook his head.

"It's a funny old game," I said, and smiled sweetly at him.

"So they say," he said, glancing unsurely at me and then looking quickly back to the road.

The outside of Sheldon House looked like a typical prison. The high brick wall surrounding it was topped with wire and close-circuit TV cameras looked down on the perimeter.

Brian left me at the gatehouse and said he'd come back in an hour. I took the briefcase and walked jauntily up to a booth by the entrance and said who I was and who I'd come to see. I was let in by a prison officer and taken through a courtyard into a reception area and asked to take a seat. Doctor Geraghy, I was told, would be down to collect me shortly.

Some minutes later a young man appeared through some swing doors. He was wearing jeans and a short-sleeved shirt, no tie. He had short hair and gold-rimmed penny glasses. In his right ear was a simple sleeper earring.

"Miss Kelly?" he said. I got up and held my hand out. I noticed the label that hung from his shirt pocket, Dr David Geraghy MD, FRC.

"Dr Geraghy," I said, surprised at his age, his ordinariness. He smiled at me and I saw he had a front tooth missing. He must have noticed me looking.

"A patient knocked it out, with his foot, a couple of weeks ago."

"Ah!" I said, embarrassed.

"It's OK. The insurance will pay for the cap. Come with me, Miss Kelly. We can talk in my office."

I picked up my briefcase and walked after him, through the swing doors and through a long office with a number of women sitting tapping at keyboards. A notice on the back of a computer monitor made me raise my eyebrows. It said, *You don't have to be mad to work here, but it helps.*

"I can't tell you a great deal about Chris Dean, Miss Kelly," David Geraghy said, when we were in his office. He was moving one of the piles of folders that seemed to cover the top of his desk. "I've only been in Sheldon for three months now, I took over from Dr Jefferson who had only been a temporary replacement for the retiring Dr Blake. I have all the notes – I put them here earlier today." He began to lift the files off a pile one by one, looking at their names. "But even with Chris's file, there won't be a lot that you don't know already. Chris was a very disturbed young man, his unhappiness possibly dating much further back than the crash, it's hard to say and we shall probably never know now, ah, here it is."

He pulled out a dog-eared file and proceeded to sit down on the corner of the desk and open it. He seemed to forget me for a moment, so I used it to jot down things that he'd already said.

"Yes," he said, eventually. "Chris's father was killed in a road accident, yes. I believe that was brought up in the trial."

He seemed to be reminding himself about who Chris was and what he'd done. I had hoped he would know those things. He continued reading and I looked around the office. It was a mess. There were at least two stained mugs in different positions on the filing cabinet and a discarded polythene wrapper from a packet of sandwiches on top of some papers. The calendar on the wall was still on July even though we were in the middle of September.

"Yes, yes, I remember this case. Chris Dean had some treatment for depression after his father was killed in a car crash."

"That's not unusual, is it? For someone to be depressed if a parent dies."

"Yes, of course, but this was not just depression. It was months of not sleeping, not eating, odd behaviour. The boy took it badly."

"And when he came in here?"

"Yes, I'm just coming to that." He was flicking through the pages of the file. I noticed then Dr Geraghy's highly polished loafers. His jeans were newish as well and his shirt perfectly ironed. There was a pleasant smell coming from him as well, a brand of aftershave that I didn't recognize.

"Here. Yes." He was speaking as he was reading. It was clear that he didn't have a clue about the details of the case. "Chris came here with partial amnesia. He had blacked out a period of weeks that led up to the crash."

"Did he have treatment for that?" I said.

"After a fashion, yes." Dr Geraghy put the file down for a moment. "You see, Miss Kelly, when prisoners are referred to Sheldon House they are examined and usually prescribed a variety of treatment. A bit of everything, to see what works; individual therapy, group therapy, shock treatment, drugs. Christopher was originally prescribed a range of drugs and some group therapy. Here," he picked up the file again and read for a few seconds, "Dr Marshall did some work with him then, for about four months but he left. Chris responded quite well, began to remember some fragments of his lost time. It looks like Dr Willis took over then…"

Dr Jefferson, Dr Blake, Dr Marshall, Dr Willis. How many doctors had Christopher seen?

"He had a couple of bad episodes as well, during his second year here. He began to develop acute claustrophobia. Hadn't shown any signs of it when he first came. He got hysterical about being in his room, or any small room. The visits seemed to trigger it off. That's not unusual. Visits represent the real world to our patients. Once the visitors have gone, in this case it was usually his twin sister I believe, once they've gone, the patient is then faced with the fact of their own imprisonment. The attacks got so bad that we had to sleep him in a dormitory which is always unsatisfactory."

"Why?"

"It means the administration of more drugs, to help them sleep, to calm them down. Patients usually find it difficult being in contact with other severely disturbed people."

I felt a shiver that didn't materialize.

"There were also a few delusional episodes."

"Yes?"

"In his last year here. It appears, from these records, that he would be coming along OK, responding to group therapy and suddenly begin to see things. Giant cockroaches, Dr Willis said, dozens of small spiders running over him. He began to insist, once, that he was trapped inside a small black box that was full of ants. These things seem laughable, I know…"

He stopped and looked at me. His eyes were smiling, his face was pleasing, attractive. He had an easy manner. He was someone who would never fall apart like Christopher Dean had. Ants, spiders, cockroaches. None of it seemed laughable to me.

"Did Christopher get any help with this?"

"He was prescribed an efficient tranquillizer, I believe."

"But any actual therapy? To find out the causes of it?"

"Miss Kelly," he said, with a sigh. "All the inmates have therapy, but you do have to remember that we are a part of the prison service here. Our main job is to contain difficult and often disturbed prisoners."

"And cure them?"

"It's not as simple as that. I wish it was." David Geraghy glanced down at his watch for a micro-second. "We do what we can, Miss Kelly. Chris was a sick young man. He'd had years of mental illness. He seemed like a typical victim, afraid that everyone was out to get him. I even remember reading some odd reports about him from his boarding school." He began to flick through the pages of the file on his lap. "I remember seeing them here."

"Is that usual? For a school to send reports to a prison?"

"Absolutely. If they have something relevant to say. Now where did I put them?" He was thumbing through sheet after sheet of dusty paper. "I don't seem to be able to locate them for the moment."

"Can you remember what…"

"The point that I was making," he interrupted, "is that Chris's problems date back a lot further than the accident he was involved in." He closed the file and laid it on the desk behind him. He then looked down at his jeans, and with his thumb and forefinger picked a tiny bit of fluff off his knee.

"What about the journal? That was your idea, wasn't it?" I said, trying to hold on to the conversation.

"Yes, it was," he beamed. "It was an attempt to help Chris to analyse his own thoughts, to try and build up a picture. It's a technique I've developed for a number of my patients."

"What did you make of the things he wrote in it?" I said, looking straight at him.

"Significant," he nodded his head, "very significant." He looked at his watch. It had a flat gold face and I was reminded of Sarah Dean's watch that had hands but no numbers. Expensive, just like his clothes. His office was a tip but he was well groomed.

"Thanks for your time," I said. I was willing to

bet he'd never looked at the journal, never bothered to read what Christopher had written.

"Anytime," he said, smiling widely and showing the gap where his front tooth had been kicked out, "and I'll look out those school reports for you when I get a minute."

He walked me back to the reception area the same way that we'd come in. I sorted out one of my cards and gave it to him. "In case you think of anything that might be important," I said. He took the card and was about to say something when his attention was taken by a girl in a pair of yellow leggings and a gold top.

"Sandra! How was Turkey?" he said and in the same breath, "Thanks, Miss Kelly," offering his hand for a brief shake before he turned and followed the smiling woman into the office. A prison officer appeared from nowhere and showed me out to the front entrance, and then into the car park where I could see Brian's car across the way.

I was filled with dismay. Christopher Dean had had a miserable time in prison. Had that been part of the punishment? Isn't that what Billy had wanted? What all of us had wanted? Would I have cared if I hadn't been trying to prove Billy innocent of his murder?

I got into the car. Brian was reading a fanzine called *On A Mission From Earth*. He glanced up at me. "How was it?" he said.

"Oh, you know, a regular madhouse," I said and sat down, pulling my seat belt out roughly with annoyance.

15
Keeping In Touch

Brian Martin dropped me off at the office on his way back to the market. We arranged to meet after he'd finished work, about six. He'd been chatty in the car on the way back, going over all the things that had been said. He'd given my arm a squeeze as I got out of the car and tooted the horn a couple of times as he drove off. I found myself smiling foolishly as I dodged across the road, my briefcase in hand, avoiding, at the last minute, a courier motorcyclist who shouted something rude after me.

I hadn't been in the office for a couple of days. There was a pile of letters on the floor by the letterbox and the answer-phone was blinking insistently. I imagined my uncle's face if he saw it and felt my mood changing. I also wondered what he'd think about me working on Billy's case. I pushed it to the back of my mind. I took my mum's jacket off and hung it carefully on a hanger. I picked up the mail and my briefcase and went into my uncle's office. I sat down in his chair for a minute and took a few deep breaths. I couldn't afford to get into a flap.

I opened the mail and sorted through it. There was nothing urgent, some bills and a couple of letters from companies supplying information that Tony had asked for. There were six phone messages. I got some files out, rang a couple of solicitors back and dealt with their enquiries and made a note of the other calls. There was nothing that wouldn't wait until Tony came back. I put the kettle on in the outer office and went back into Tony's office and sat down to look at my notes.

While in prison Christopher Dean had been claustrophobic. I remembered that day when he came to see me. One of his memories was of a growing fear of darkness, he'd said, a fear of being *closed in*. In prison he'd become afraid of ants, spiders and cockroaches. He'd been a collector of them, Josie had said. In his journal he'd drawn them, all over the place.

These were classic phobias, I was sure. Many mentally unstable people exhibited such symptoms. Often the cause was something quite different.

But Christopher was also afraid of his step-brother and, I tapped my pen against my lip, his sister Sarah.

I remembered her mother's words: *I know that you forced Chris to make a new will.*

I shook my head. It didn't make sense. Christopher had been a dependent, weak character. Sarah had looked after him. She had been keen to get a reconciliation between Billy and her brother. She had stood by him throughout the trial. She had visited him for three years while he'd been in Sheldon House, looked at by a procession of doctors.

And yet wasn't it after those very visits that Chris had got worse? I flicked through my notes. *C got hysterical about being in any small room, visits triggered it off.*

But Sarah Dean was helping me.

I sat back in my uncle's chair, a low creak coming from the springs. I reached out for my cup of tea and discovered that it wasn't there. I hadn't made it for myself yet. I'd been so absorbed with the case that I'd forgotten.

The phone rang then and I picked it up. I got my pen ready, expecting to have to take notes for my uncle.

"Pat, is that you?" It was Billy.

"Billy! How are you?" I raised my voice, speaking delightedly as though I hadn't seen him in weeks.

"All right, all right. I got this phone card so I thought I'd ring."

"What's it like?" I said, and then wished I hadn't.

"You mean prison? You know, loads of bars and kids walking round with their feet chained together."

"You know what I mean!" I said. I didn't really know what I meant. I really wanted him to say that the food wasn't too bad, that he'd read up on his rights and that he'd made some friends.

"It's miserable. It's dirty and there's this constant smell of body odour. Apart from that I'm fitting in nicely."

"But you got a phone card," I said, as though that was something on the bright side.

"Patsy, how's the case going?" He said it quietly, in a voice that was empty of expectations.

"It's going well." I said it in a businesslike way. I then went on to give him a summary of the things I'd found out. I left out my budding doubt about Sarah Dean. He spoke from time to time, mostly *um* or *probably* or *don't read too much into it*. I kept going, though. I told him that Heather and Tony were due back soon. He didn't sound very reassured so I asked him to talk to me about the night of the murder again, to go through it, step by step. I clicked my tape recorder on and held it close to the mouthpiece.

"There's not much I haven't told you already. I

got there about sevenish, I suppose. Megan said that Sarah would be ready in a minute, asked me to wait in the kitchen. I did, so…"

"Where were you going that night? I mean, what was the arrangement? Were you going out on a date?"

"A date? Patsy. Are you in a time warp? We were going to the cinema."

I felt foolish. I ignored his comment.

"So you weren't involved romantically?"

"Sort of…"

"You don't sound very sure."

"I suppose I'm not. You know how it is, Patsy. You don't always know how these things will turn out." I didn't answer. He was referring to *us*, I was sure. I had a sudden spurt of guilt about Brian Martin. I let him talk on. "It might have developed, who knows. Look," he was stumbling on his words trying to explain himself, "I felt sorry for her. I liked her. She was nice company, easy to be with."

"And very nice-looking," I said and then bit my lip. Why had I said that?

"And that. She was lonely, she said. She kept ringing me up, asking me to go places, said she needed someone outside the family to talk to."

"She kept ringing you up?"

"Yes. I was surprised – that's an understatement – I was flattered."

"But *she* rang you?"

137

"Yes, three or four times."

I wrote it down.

"She appeared anyway a few minutes after I got there. She said she was just popping out to say good night to Chris and then we were going to go. Megan was around, I think, although she went off upstairs somewhere."

"And Sarah went out to the summer house?"

"Yes. She came back into the kitchen, said something about Christopher having fallen asleep. She said she was going upstairs for her bag."

"Then?"

"I was finishing my drink, reading the paper, some article about electric cars. It was a while, really, I can't exactly say how long, ten, fifteen minutes. At one point I got up and walked to the door of the kitchen. I remember I kept thinking that we'd be late for the film. That was when I heard the whining sound that I told you about. Only – I've been thinking about it – it wasn't Christopher, it wasn't human. I've been playing it over and over in my head, you know, and I think it was an animal crying, whimpering."

"An animal?"

"Yes, I can't explain it. An animal. Anyway. I went out in the garden, then into the summer house and you know the rest."

A series of beeps interrupted him and then I heard, "Patsy, I've run out of units. Send me some phone cards and I'll ring…" but his last words were cut off.

I sighed and put the phone down. Then I pressed the rewind button on the recorder. Sarah Dean had rung Billy, not the other way round. I was sure that she had said to me that it was Billy who rang her. I picked up a pen and got ready to hear the tape over again.

Sarah Dean had gone out to the summer house minutes before Chris was killed. Had Billy told that to the police?

The tiniest bit of exhilaration was nudging me. There were new things in what Billy had said. All I had to do was pick them out and link them up with what I already knew.

I clicked the replay button and listened as his voice told me the story again.

I got down to the market at about six. I'd just posted four phone cards to Billy when I turned and walked towards the car park where I said I'd meet Brian. I was buzzing with excitement and plans. At last I had an opening, a way into the case. I couldn't wait to tell Brian. Apart from this I was looking forward to just seeing him again.

How different things were from when I first met him. How he'd irritated me then with his silly chat-up lines that seemed to come from a hundred old films. He'd changed, though, grown up. I'd treated him badly, I remembered that. At least this time I was being honest with him.

He came along about five minutes after I'd got there.

In the car I told him about Billy's phone call. I also told him that I planned to go up to the house in Hampstead that very evening.

"Because you think Sarah killed her brother?" he said. He raised his eyebrows in an incredulous way.

"I'm not jumping that far, not yet. There's inconsistencies, though. I need to talk to her, to iron it out. If only I had contacts with the police. I'd know then if she'd explained about going out to the summer house to see Chris. There may be a perfectly good explanation for it. Could she have known that Jamie Kent was on his way round? Could *she* have taken the book?"

"But why?"

"Because there was something bad in it about her?"

"This is silly, Pat. She's the one who wanted you on her brother's case. Why would she want a private detective if she had plans to murder him?"

"Maybe she didn't plan it. Maybe she only decided when she realized he was remembering things. Uncomfortable things that involved her in some way."

"But why would she have wanted you to look into the case if she had something to hide from three years ago? And what about Jamie Kent? Is he involved too?"

"I don't know!" I said with sudden frustration. Brian had an answer for everything. There was an icy silence for a minute and I stared out of the wind-screen with annoyance. After a few seconds I heard him moving about in his seat and felt his hand on my shoulder.

"Patsy, if you just wanted me to agree with you, to say yes at the end of everything, you should have told me. I thought you wanted my opinion." His voice was soft, calm. I found myself looking hard at the sticker that said *Follow the Hammers*. He was right. I let the tension go from my shoulders and leaned back on the seat.

"I'm sorry, you're right. It's just that I feel like I'm working blindfolded…"

I stopped speaking, though, because Brian had leant towards me and was kissing me lightly on the ear, his mouth pausing for a moment, his face buried in my hair, his breath on my skin.

I closed my eyes as a tingle crept up through my neck. Then I turned and held his face and kissed him hard on the mouth, my lips sideways, my tongue just touching his. In the back of my head I could hear the car seat creak as he leant forward and put both his arms around me, his fingers pressing into my back. It seemed to go on for a long time, neither of us breaking off, my face locked into his, a swooning feeling in the pit of my stomach.

How did we both breathe? I don't know. I wasn't thinking about it. My mind was a blank sheet of paper but my skin had come alive with feeling.

A sudden knocking broke us apart. A hand rapping, hard on the passenger's window of the car. I looked around. It was one of the market traders, a big dark man with a tattoo of a lion on his arm. He was making lewd gestures and laughing with his friends as they walked off. I felt myself getting embarrassed but Brian was laughing, leaning back in the driver's seat, stretching his arms as though he'd just got up.

"It's all right, Patsy," he said, turning the key in the ignition. "It's me they're laughing at, not you."

I laughed uneasily, my fingers playing with my ear.

"Hampstead, then," he said, and we drove off.

16
Search

We got there about seven-thirty. Megan, the maid, answered the door. I was surprised to see her back at work. Sarah Dean was out, due back about eight, she said. Pulling on Brian's arm and walking past her I said we'd wait. We had important things to discuss with Sarah, I said. We stood in the hall for a moment and I found my attention focusing on the stairs. Sarah Dean's bedroom was on the second floor. It was the only place in the house where I hadn't had so much as a quick peek.

Megan looked unsure about letting us come in. After a few moments she led us into the living room.

"How are you feeling, Megan?" I said. It came to me then that it was almost a week to the hour when she had walked into the summer house and found Christopher's body.

"Better, much better now, thank you."

She looked pale, though, and kept putting her fingernails up to her mouth as though she were going to bite them, then changed her mind. I noticed that she was wearing her own clothes, jeans and a floral shirt, not the dark skirt and white blouse she'd been wearing the first day we came.

"It must have been awful for you, finding Christopher like that."

"Yes," she said, lifting her fingers to her mouth. I remembered that Josie said that she had lost her own brother a year before. Did that make it worse, I wondered?

"Is it long, until you go back to college?" I said, wary of asking her about it. I was almost a stranger to her. I had no right to pry into her family grief.

"A couple of weeks," she said, smiling awkwardly. She was moving about on the spot, looking uncomfortable. Perhaps it wasn't the done thing to chat to her employer's guests.

"What are you studying?" Brian said.

"Drama, well, performing arts really."

"That's interesting," I said, trying to put her more at ease. I looked at my watch. There was about twenty minutes or so until Sarah came back. Would that give me time to go up and have a quick look in her bedroom, through her things?

144

"Can I get you some tea, while you're waiting for Sarah?" Megan said, taking a secretive look at her watch.

"That would be nice," Brian said and sat down on a sofa, picking up a glossy magazine from the coffee table in front of him.

I watched the living-room door close and then I told Brian what I was going to do.

"But what exactly are you looking for?" he said in a loud whisper.

"Don't know," I said.

Maybe, deep down, it was just that I wanted to have a good look at Sarah Dean's clothes.

The room was pristinely tidy. It was decorated in a Laura Ashley style, heavily flowered wallpaper with contrasting borders. The curtains on the window were of the same design, pulled up at each side the way theatre curtains sometimes look. The bed was made out of a highly varnished wood with off-white linen pillows and a bedspread. On the corner of each pillow were the initials SD. Sarah Dean. It reminded me of her headed notepaper. She liked people to know who she was.

I hadn't really got a clue about what I was looking for. The red book? A secret diary with Sarah's plans to murder her brother outlined in it? I began to lose confidence. Sarah had *helped* me. What if she came back and found me rifling through her things? I almost turned round and went back downstairs.

Something stopped me, though, and I set about looking round the room.

The wall opposite the windows was covered by a fitted wardrobe. It must have been twelve to fifteen feet wide. I thought briefly of my own little wardrobe at home, things falling out of it every time I opened a door, my hats piled up in boxes on the top.

There were four separate doors and I opened all of them. It was packed full with expensive-looking clothes, coats, dresses, skirts, trousers – there must have been about fifty or sixty items hung there. Along the floor were shoes and boots. I flicked my eyes across and shook my head with irritation. How could one person own so many different things to wear? Sarah Dean could probably go for weeks without wearing the same pair of shoes twice.

I stood back in the middle of the room. I wasn't sure where to go next. Opposite her bed was a bookcase. I ran my fingers along the shelves. Everything was so tidy, so organized. I opened some drawers but all I saw were neat piles of underwear, T-shirts, leggings and unopened packets of tights.

Surely Sarah had a drawer that was full of odds and ends?

I opened the wardrobe again and looked through. It was all still the same and I might have closed the doors again if I hadn't noticed three shoe boxes on the floor, underneath some black boots and yellow sandals. I crouched over and eased the lid off one of them and my face broke into a smile. This was where Sarah kept her paperwork. Odd, I thought. I would have expected something more substantial, an antique desk or a lacquered writing box.

I sat cross-legged on the floor and took the boxes out. The first one was full of photographs and papers, old birthday cards and tickets for what looked like theatre performances. The second box had what looked like old school reports and headed letters from a firm of solicitors. The third was full of receipts. They were from places like Libertys and Harrods and there were even odd ones from Marks and Spencer.

I went back to the box with the photographs, picked up a bundle and flicked through. There were several old ones, taken when the twins were much younger, ten or eleven, say. I turned over the back of the photograph to see Sarah Dean's neat hand-writing, Christopher and Sarah, France '85. There were half a dozen of the pair in various positions. Flicking through I found several of an older man, maybe Sarah's father. They were old photos, awkward poses beside a youthful (and thinner) Mrs Kent (Mrs Dean, then) and the twins at a much younger age.

I had a quick flick through the box and a white envelope caught my eye. On the outside were the words *The Adams Family!!!* I smiled, thinking of the old TV programme, but then I remembered that Adams had been the surname of the woman who Sarah's dad had got involved with. The woman who was killed in the crash with him. I tipped them out into my hand and had a moment's shock when I looked at them. There were about a dozen, some of the couple, Mr Dean and Mrs Adams, some of the twins with Mrs Adams and another young girl who looked to be the same age as Sarah. The disturbing thing was that all the pictures of Mrs Adams had a black cross over her face. It was some kind of marker or felt-tip and it looked striking, a solid X, as if someone were planning to start a game of noughts and crosses. The only picture that didn't have the X on it was one of Sarah and Mrs Adams's daughter. They were both fancy-dress fairies and were smiling at the camera. Mrs Adams's daughter had vivid red hair and she was smiling widely, a wand in her hand, her other hand holding Sarah's. On the back were the words, Sarah and Philippa, Christmas.

Sarah Dean must have hated her father's woman friend. I wondered why. I kept a couple of the photos and replaced the others. There was another photo though, stuck down in the corner of the envelope. I struggled to get it out. It was two of a strip of four photos. It was Sarah, younger, her hair shorter and a boy, his hair dark, his face pleasant. They were both smiling. I turned the photos over.

On the back were the words, *To Sarah, I love you, Jamie*.

I sat back and felt several pieces of the mystery suddenly fall into place, I almost *heard* them fall into place. Sarah Dean had been involved with Jamie Kent. *Romantically* involved with him. Whatever had happened three years before might have involved her as well.

I imagined Brian's voice, though: *well, why did she want a private investigator on the case if she had something to hide?*

But had she really wanted a private investigator? She had asked me, it was true, in front of Christopher. What if she only wanted Christopher to think she was getting a private investigator? It was, after all, during the days when he was changing his will in favour of her.

And why ask me? Sarah and Christopher had pots of money. They could have gone to any firm of investigators. And why wait three years? Why hadn't Sarah got an investigator as soon as Christopher was arrested?

I looked at the photos again. Jamie Kent was a good-looking boy. I could see why Sarah might have been interested in him.

I then remembered coming round to see her the day before. She hadn't been interested at all in my investigating the case until I had mentioned Christopher's possible phone call to Jamie Kent.

She'd gone off then and phoned her mother. It was then that she seemed to make a decision to help me. Why was that? Was it to keep me from going to the police? To keep her informed of what I was finding out? Did that mean she had the book, the journal?

I remembered her coming down the stairs dressed to kill in order to go to the police station on my behalf. She'd had a bag over her shoulder, big enough to hide a book in. Had she taken the journal out of the house then, in case I should stumble across it?

The bang of the front door jolted me out of my thoughts. I stuffed most of the photos back into the shoe box and put them back in the wardrobe. Closing the doors quietly I stood up quickly, tucking the photos I'd kept into my jacket pocket. I took a quick look around the bedroom to make sure I hadn't left any mess. Then I crept across the landing, went into the toilet and flushed it.

The unanswered question still hung in the air. What had happened three years before? Was it something so bad that Sarah and Jamie Kent had murdered Christopher in order to stop him remembering it?

Had the business with Billy been a part of it all? Had Sarah deliberately set Billy up, brought him up to the house, had him there so that when Christopher was killed it would look as though he had done it?

I shook my head. I was letting my imagination

run away with me. I didn't even know, with any certainty, that they had killed Christopher at all. All I really knew was that they had been involved with each other and that Sarah had kept quiet about it.

I walked slowly back out and, down the stairs, I could hear Sarah Dean's voice from the living room. I walked in brusquely and said, "Hi, Sarah. I just thought I'd come and tell you about Dr Geraghy. This is Brian, by the way, my friend."

She was standing stiffly with her back to the fireplace. In one hand she was still holding her car keys, the giant "S" hanging down like a snake from her fingers. I ignored the coldness emanating from her, and went and sat next to Brian. I recounted the visit to Dr Geraghy and told her about Billy's phone call and most of what he'd said. She agreed that she had gone out to the summer house to see Chris on the night he was murdered. He'd taken a tranquillizer, though, and was having a nap so she hadn't been able to speak to him. He often took tranquillizers, she said, looking mildly irritated that I should have asked her at all.

All the time I was watching her face. She looked bored, as though she'd had enough of the whole thing. Although she was very still I did notice her foot tapping rapidly.

"So I'm back to where I started, really. What I need to find is the red book. I'm sure that's the key."

In the distance the phone began to ring. Sarah's

attention was taken by it, her eyes swivelling away towards the door. I found myself looking at her keys. Her car keys. The red book was the *key* to the whole thing. If Sarah had taken the book out with her on the day I was looking around the house might she have left it *in her car*?

"Sarah," Megan's voice came from downstairs, "someone for you on the telephone."

On the coffee table just feet away from her was a black push-button phone.

"Excuse me, I'll just take it downstairs," Sarah said, ignoring it. She left her keys on the mantelpiece and the door closed gently behind her.

I looked at the car keys and made a snap decision.

"Watch Sarah. Make excuses for me. I'll be back in a minute."

"Why?" I heard Brian's voice but I ignored it, picked up the keys and went straight out into the hall and headed for the front door.

The keys fitted the blue hatchback that was parked outside. I opened the driver's door and knelt in on the seat to look around. One glance told me that there was nothing in there. It was as neat and tidy as Sarah's bedroom. I went quickly round to the back and opened the hatch. There was just the spare tyre, nothing else. I was about to close it down when I thought of something. I lifted up the plastic fabric that covered the tyre and looked through the hole in the middle.

There it was. The red book. I clenched my fist with delight.

I lifted up the tyre and took it out, holding it carefully as though it were some expensive antique.

I couldn't believe my luck. I looked guiltily round the street. *Car thief* must have been written all over my face. There was no sign of anyone so I closed the car up, put the red book under my jacket and slipped quietly back into the house. Brian was in the hall waiting for me but there was no sign of Sarah. I left the car keys on a table in the hall.

"Sarah's got a headache," he said. "She's gone upstairs to lie down."

"Did she notice I was gone?" I whispered, looking around.

"No, she didn't even come back in the room. Megan told me."

"Oh."

"She had an interesting phone call. I'll tell you in the car."

In the car I showed Brian the book. I was talking ten to the dozen, speeding on with excitement, flicking through the pages. There was something in it that fell on to my lap when I opened it, a group photograph from school, at least a part of one. It was like a bookmark. Turning it over I could see Christopher Dean's face, younger, in a school uniform, surrounded by other boys.

I was so relieved that I'd got away with it! I'd searched her room and her car and she hadn't known! I was feeling pleased with myself, thrilled with my own performance. I couldn't wait to get home and pore over the book, to see if it revealed anything.

Suddenly, without warning, Brian braked, pulled the car over to the side of the road and sat looking at me.

"Have you finished?" he said.

"What?"

"Have you finished talking? Only I'd like to get a word in, about the phone call."

"Sorry!" I said in an indignant tone of voice. I felt a flush of embarrassment and my hands clamped over the book on my lap.

"I picked the phone up in the living room and listened in to Sarah's phone call."

I raised my eyebrows at this. What with Brian's dad being a policeman and all.

"It was Jamie Kent she was talking to, I'm sure."

I opened my mouth to speak but decided against it.

"It was very secretive, like he didn't say his name. He mentioned 'Mum' and that 'bloody' book. He asked whether the police were looking for him. What do you think of that!"

Putting the red book on the floor I got the photo of Sarah and Jamie out of my pocket and handed it to Brian. I said nothing all the while. He switched on the inside light of the car and held it up. The two lovers looked back at us, their faces touching. He turned it over. *To Sarah, I love you, Jamie.*

"They're meeting, tomorrow morning, on Hampstead Heath. Ten o'clock," he said.

I kept quiet. I didn't want to be accused of talking too much again. I picked up Brian's hand, though, and kissed it gently.

Now we're getting somewhere, I thought.

17
The Journal

Brian picked me up about nine the next morning. There was a grim silence in the car, neither of us needing to say much. We'd already spoken at length late the previous evening when I'd rung him to tell him what I'd read in the journal. It had been upsetting, disturbing. I had had great difficulty getting to sleep and in the end had got up at two-twenty and made myself a cup of tea.

As I'd sat at the kitchen table, hugging the warm mug and staring out into the pitch dark of the garden, I'd felt uneasy, the silence of the deep night thick and solid.

I'd felt this overwhelming sympathy for Christopher Dean. A boy who'd been a classic victim; weak, easily manipulated and bullied. I'd picked up the photograph of him that I'd found inside the journal. He'd been a frail-looking school kid, smaller and thinner than the others around him. All the same he'd been smiling, his arm around the boy next to him, perhaps his best friend. Did boys have *best friends*? I tried to remember Billy when he was younger but I couldn't.

In the car, on the long road back to Hampstead Heath that morning, I let the book lie on my lap, innocent-looking, its bright red covers giving no hint of what was inside.

I can't say that I'd been shocked. I'd been expecting something unpleasant so I'd braced myself. When I'd told Brian he'd just said, *What a cowardly thing to do.* As though it was as simple as that; two boys, involved in a struggle and one doing something underhand. My own view was more damning: it hadn't just been cowardly, it had been downright cruel.

"Where exactly did you say they were meeting?" I said to Brian, as we pulled up at some lights.

"Kenwood House. It's an old stately home on the Heath. I looked it up last night. It's got a cafeteria. They're meeting in there."

Meeting in a cafeteria; it didn't seem quite grand enough for Sarah Dean.

My opinion of Sarah Dean had plummeted. She had known what had happened to her brother. She had been aware of the deterioration of relations between Jamie Kent and Christopher. She was his sister, for goodness' sake, couldn't she have stopped it?

"Were there any dates in the book?" Brian said after a while.

"No."

There were no dates because it wasn't like a diary with a neat account on every page of that day's events.

"Why don't you read it over to me, just so's I'm clear about it all. We'll be there soon," he said.

I opened the book and turned past the inside cover that had *Sorry Billy* written over and over again, past the pages of insects and the incomplete scribbles, the bits of the jigsaw that Christopher had remembered but hadn't been able to make sense of. I put the school photograph to one side, its edges slightly jagged where it had been cut from a larger picture. I turned to the most recent pages that he'd written on. I'd highlighted all the important bits in a flourescent pink. There must have been three pages of scrawling notes, written in a rush, as though Christopher might forget it all before he'd written it down.

I read slowly and without much expression in my voice.

The sauna.

It was the only place. Soundproof. The door could be locked. Who could hear the cries? No one – that was the point.

Inside it was dark, blacker than anywhere. Like deep water down at the very bottom of the sea. No air, nothing to breathe, just pitch black.

And they would be there. Somewhere in the dark. In a corner, their silk stretching from one wall to the other, being pulled from side to side. A perfect web, big enough to catch anything, even a boy.

The pain. First of all being hit, held tight, pushed around, shoved hard against the wood on the outside. The voice that seems to come from inside the chest, husky, don't, please don't, no don't.

Thrown in, stumbling, falling, the pain of a fist on the head like a hot needle, then the door shuts and it's darker than the grave. A long tunnel, only no light at the end.

And they're there in the corners, silently padding on their feet, like crabs moving across the floor. The heat of the body unsettling them. There's a shivering because they're not imprisoned any more, they're roaming free. It's the boy who's captured.

Are those the eyes? Can the eyes be seen? Like the lights on a train that is far away, miles away, two red pin pricks. Can they be seen? Or is it imagination?

The night is long. It lasts for years, for a boy's lifetime, like it will never end. In the corner there's the waiting, and after a while the darkness thins and is only like a mist. Then it's possible to see around the edges, the shapes. The door locked firmly, the square of the window is there. Slide by it, up to it, my skin close and there through the glass is the screaming boy his mouth open wide enough to swallow all the spiders in the world...

She comes, the door is open. She knew, she knew what it did to me she knew and she's there with her hair like the silk from a spider's web. She's shouting and there's tears but I can't stay. I have to run, I have to get away. Up the stairs, out of the darkness, the light hurts my eyes.

The car is there and it's an escape because I mustn't be caught. It's too terrible, to spend a night of your life in a dark box.

I've driven it before, I know where everything is but it's dark again. The street's like a long tunnel only there's no train just the eyes coming out of the darkness and I mustn't let them get to me. Not red any more, just yellow eyes, staring, coming closer and the only thing to do is to run them over to get rid of them.

Then it's as quiet as the graveyard only I can hear a bird wailing, coming closer, to pick it up off the ground. The giant spider that's dead at my feet.

I stopped reading and closed the book.

"This sauna," Brian said after a while. "It's in the cellar?"

"Basement playroom. It's been locked for years Josie said, but I guess Jamie Kent must have got hold of a key."

"And the spiders were Christopher's."

"Yes. I guess it's one thing having them as pets and another being locked in a dark box with them."

"You think Sarah was part of it?"

"I don't know. I wonder if she could have been. I think she was involved with Jamie Kent. This boy took a dislike to Christopher. Could he have been jealous of the relationship between the brother and sister?"

"What a thing to do, though."

"As I was reading it I kept thinking maybe it was a game of dares or something, you know, *I dare you to spend the night in the sauna in the dark with several large spiders for company.*"

"The spiders weren't poisonous, though?"

"No. But would it matter? If you were a weak, impressionable boy. Someone who had already experienced mental illness. Christopher had said he had a great fear of meeting Jamie Kent. Now we know why."

We were driving along by the side of the Heath and we both lapsed into our own thoughts. I wondered how Sarah could live with herself. Her boyfriend guilty of torturing her brother, sending him fleeing into the night when he took the car and smashed into Billy's parents.

Had she thought that Christopher would never remember what happened?

And when he did, had she rung Jamie and told him to come over and get rid of her brother?

There was the money as well. The will that had been recently changed.

We parked in the car park attached to Kenwood House and walked the short distance to the stately home and its restaurant. Looking round I could see the grounds stretching for ever, backing on to Hampstead Heath. The place was covered with people walking their pedigree dogs; Afghan hounds, spaniels, collies, standard poodles. At one point I stepped aside to avoid a red setter that was gambolling towards me. I was reminded for a moment of the dog I had seen walking along the street on the night that Christopher had been murdered.

Brian nudged me. About twenty feet ahead I could see the back of Sarah Dean, walking ahead of us towards the café. She had an arm around the shoulder of a young man beside her, Jamie Kent.

He was smaller than I'd thought he'd be, shorter than Sarah by a couple of inches. I could only see his back, his brown hair curling over a denim jacket. Sarah, walking beside him, was wearing a long beige mac and dark trousers.

We held back for a minute, letting them get ahead of us into the cafeteria.

Once inside we saw them sitting side by side at a table. Sarah was talking quietly into the young man's ear.

I was disappointed when I saw him. He looked younger than I had imagined, his face babyish almost, showing none of the cruelty and ruthlessness that I had expected. We stood for a moment before walking over to them. That was when Sarah noticed us.

"Hi, Sarah," I said. "You must be Jamie Kent. We've been looking for you."

He said nothing and I threw the book down on the table.

"There's some interesting stuff in there, Jamie. Seems things got out of hand a couple of years ago."

I sat down on a chair opposite and looked Sarah straight in the face. Brian sat next to me.

"How could you do it to him? Your own brother?"

At last she showed some reaction.

"What do you mean?" she said.

"Imprisoning him, torturing him. You must have known how unstable he was."

"You've read this," Sarah said, an edge of anger to her voice.

"Of course," I said. "Over and over."

"And you think that Jamie and me tortured Chris?"

"I think *he* did."

That's when she started to cry and Jamie Kent put his arm around her. "It's all right, Sarah," he said. "It's all over now. It's got to come out. We can't keep it back any more."

She was sobbing though, tears clinging to her face. Her cool exterior red and blotchy, even her expensive clothes and well-cut hair didn't stop her from looking pathetic. I had no sympathy for her.

Until Jamie Kent spoke.

He picked up the book with his free hand and said, looking first at Brian and then at me, "It wasn't me who locked Christopher Dean in the sauna. It was him who locked me in. For hours, in the pitch dark, with the insects. He sat outside while I begged him to let me out. I nearly went out of my mind."

18
Incarcerated

"Christopher Dean was a seriously strange kid," Jamie Kent said. He'd taken his arm away from Sarah Dean's shoulder and was leaning on the table, his hands cupped as if he were about to say a prayer. Brian and I were sitting nonplussed. Neither of us saying anything. Sarah Dean joined in.

"Right after my dad's accident, Chris fell apart, not eating, not sleeping. He was never the same."

"He didn't like me, not one bit," Jamie said. "He made that quite clear the minute I got there. He was never upfront about it. It was all in secret. Calling me names, talking about my dad and his mum, goading me all the time. He was posh, see, could speak properly. I was just a kid from a comprehensive."

Sarah continued, "I found out about Chris's treatment of Jamie and I was really angry. Chris had been involved in bullying incidents at school. At least, there'd been a suggestion that he had, never any evidence. It was all part of what he forgot, you see."

"What about Jamie?" I tried to keep her on the subject.

"Jamie and I got friendly. I used to get out of school at weekends; I wasn't supposed to but nobody ever knew. Jamie and I, we got close to each other. Chris was really nasty about it, hated me getting fond of Jamie."

"It was a crazy few weeks. In the end it was me and Sarah against Chris."

"Didn't anyone notice this little war?" I said, thinking of Josie.

"No. My mum was in France. Jamie's dad was in rehearsals and hardly ever around. Josie wouldn't have pried, anyway. I think she just saw a couple of kids playing games."

"But it got really nasty. Chris started threatening me, you know, when no one was around."

"In the end, one afternoon, he walked in on me and Jamie kissing and he flew into a rage. I told him to grow up. I exploded at him. I told him to leave me alone, that my life was none of his business."

"He went quiet for a few days, said nothing," Jamie said. "To tell the truth, I began to get a bit unnerved. Everywhere I went in the house his eyes seemed to be following me. Sarah was spending some time with a friend from school. She said she would try to come home. My dad was away. The housekeeper was hardly ever around. On the Saturday, when it all happened, I hardly saw Chris all day…"

Sarah butted in, talking across Jamie. "I couldn't get away until late. I got a mini-cab. Thirty miles. It took ages. I had to pay the driver first. Then half-way home it broke down. I had to sit and wait for *another* cab to come and pick me up."

"In the evening," Jamie continued, "I went down to the playroom to set up the snooker table. That's when I saw that the tanks were empty. The big ones where Chris kept his spiders. Just then the lights went out and the place was black. I felt this thump on the back of my neck and an arm around my chest. I tried to turn round. I knew it was him but he had me in a grip and pulled me backwards. I struggled hard and moved his arm and I half turned and felt the door of the sauna open. It surprised me. It was never allowed. It was always locked. I was distracted for a moment and he shoved me two or three times and I fell in, hitting my shoulder. I tried to get up on my feet but by the time I had he had shut the door and locked it."

I was listening breathlessly.

"I banged on the door a few times, you know,

shouting out, saying 'come on Chris, open up, the joke's over'. He'd put the basement light back on by then. I could see his face at the window, grinning. Then I remembered the spiders, missing from their tanks. I looked around me. There was a beam of light streaming through the small window and I saw one of them gliding across the floor, disappearing into the dark.

"I couldn't believe he'd done it. At first I thought it would be all right. I laughed bravely for a minute. I wasn't afraid of spiders, they were harmless big things, but all at once the light in the basement went out and the place was black. I froze, I felt like I was stuck in thick black mud unable to move, unable to see. I was so scared…"

His voice began to break and he stopped talking. Sarah Dean lifted her arm around him and he covered his face with his hands. She took up the story.

"I got home about two o'clock. I crept in, not wanting to wake Josie. I went straight up to Jamie's room. When he wasn't there I went to Chris's room, then the basement. I put the light on and found Chris crouched up in the corner, his knees bent up, his arms holding them close to his chest. He seemed to be in some sort of trance. In his hand was the key to the sauna and I looked over and saw the blackness through the window.

"When I opened the door I didn't know what I

expected to find. Jamie fell out on to the floor of the basement, his eyes staring wildly, spluttering, coughing, retching. I thought ... I didn't know what to think."

"And Christopher?"

"Chris looked wildly at me and Jamie. He started saying, *No ... no ... no*, backing away, as if, like, we were going to put *him* into that dark hole. Then he pushed me aside and ran. I wasn't interested in where he'd gone. I just wanted to help Jamie."

"And the spiders?"

"I don't know. I closed the door and locked it. It's never been opened since. I wasn't interested in the spiders. I was just interested in Jamie."

I couldn't understand it. I sat back, confusion written all over my face. I picked up the book and my eyes scanned the bits that I had highlighted. I'd been wrong. Jamie Kent had been the victim, not Christopher Dean.

"I'll get some tea," I heard Brian's voice say.

The spiders had been entombed in the sauna.

The tea was steaming and we all drank it in silence. Eventually, after letting it all settle in my head, I said, "When I read it in the journal it sounded as though Christopher *himself* had been the victim."

"I know. I've looked at it over and over myself," Sarah said. "I think he wrote it like that because in some terrible way he had tried to put himself in

Jamie's position. He was so ashamed of himself he tried to *experience* what Jamie had gone through."

"Or else," Jamie Kent said, "he wrote it like that because after having done it to me it became the thing he was most afraid of anyone doing to him. That's why he was afraid of me. He thought I would get my own back. Lock him in some dark place. He was tortured by imagining what it would be like."

It was a less charitable explanation than that given by Sarah. I didn't say anything but I wasn't sure which of the two I believed.

"Why didn't you tell the police?"

"I couldn't. I couldn't tell them what sort of a person my brother was," Sarah said.

"What about you?" I said to Jamie Kent. Surely he had wanted some retribution for the way that he'd been treated?

He shook his head. "As soon as I'd pulled myself together Sarah got a taxi and took me back to my mother's house. I didn't want to be there any more. Sarah knew that. The next thing was that my dad came and told me that Chris had been involved in an accident. That two people had been killed."

"We didn't want to complicate matters. When it was clear that Chris had forgotten it all, we wanted to do that as well. We even decided not to see each other again."

"Chris was sent to prison for three years. He was being punished anyway." Jamie said it quietly.

"But when he came out? Weren't you afraid that he would remember?"

"I was taking it day by day," Sarah said. "There was no point in worrying about something that might never happen."

"Why did you take him back, after what he'd done?"

"He was my brother. I cared about him whatever."

"And Billy?"

"Whatever my brother did to Jamie Kent he did not mean to kill Billy's parents. I wanted some forgiveness for him, for that at least."

"Why did you ask Patsy to take on the case?"

"To keep Chris happy. I had no intention of getting anyone to look into his case."

"Why didn't you just tell him?"

"I was afraid of what the truth would do to him. He was always so weak, you see. Prison life hadn't helped that. He was sick and I wanted to take care of him."

"And on the night of the murder. Did you take the book?"

"Yes, I went out to the summer house to speak to him but he was lying asleep on the sofa. It was the last time I saw him alive. I didn't even see his face, it was flat into the pillow. The book was lying on the floor. I picked it up and brought it in. I intended to look through it. I often did that."

"What were you going to do with it?"

"Get rid of it, I don't know, keep it. After he was dead it was all I had left of him."

I looked straight at Jamie. "Did you go up to the house on that night, after he'd rung you?"

"I did. He rang me about five, I suppose. He was in tears, unhappy, said he remembered it all and he was sorry and would I please go and see him. So I said I would. I went to the house but I got cold feet. I'd never been there again after that awful night. Then I saw this Jaguar pull up and this young guy get out and go into the house. That's when I knew I couldn't face Sarah, so I went round the side and into the garden. I could see the summer house lights. I knew that Chris would be down there. I was building myself up to going to see him but I just couldn't. Then I started to hear all these noises, a sort of whining, like a dog. I froze for a while, then I heard this scream and saw a woman running out of the summer house up the back garden... I just waited until the crowd was big enough in the street and I slipped away."

They were leaning against each other, Sarah Dean and Jamie Kent, both their faces blotchy from crying. They didn't look like murderers, either of them. I pictured Jamie creeping through the bushes in the garden, watching the commotion, waiting for a moment to slip away.

"What about this?" I held the school photo up to Sarah.

"I don't know. It's part of Christopher's last school photo. I didn't know he had it. It must have been among his prison things because I've never seen it before."

I put it back into the book. That was when Brian spoke up.

"Did you say you heard a dog whining in the garden, when you were hiding?"

"Yeah, only for a minute…"

"Patsy, didn't you say that Billy Rogers said he heard an animal whining? That's how come he went out to the summer house."

"Yes," I said, sitting up.

"Well," Brian seemed disconcerted by my eagerness, "well, that's a coincidence. Two people hearing a dog, at that moment. Whose dog was it?"

Whose dog was it?

The man with the red setter came into my head. Walking along the dark street, his dog in front of him, his face covered by the hood of his sweatshirt. There was my mum and I, sitting in her car, talking about her sad love life only minutes before the maid had discovered Christopher's body. The dog had been distinctive, a red setter. The house he had gone into was called *Cherry Tree Villa*.

I stood up. Sarah and Jamie looked at me.

"Where are you going now?" I said to both of them.

"I don't know. We haven't decided," Sarah said.

"Before you do anything, promise me one thing. Take Jamie to the police and tell them everything you've told me. Everything. I don't know if it will help but it's got to come out, all of it, no matter how bad it makes Christopher look."

"Where are you going?" Sarah said. Jamie and Brian were looking at me closely. I wasn't sure, it may have been nothing, but it was worth a try.

"I'm going to see a man about a dog," I said.

19
Dizzy

Cherry Tree Villa looked quiet and calm as we drove up and parked outside. It was a big house in a country-cottage style and in the front garden were several trees, cherry, I supposed.

I wasn't really sure how to proceed. I wanted to talk to the man who had walked the dog on the night of Christopher's murder. Two people who had been in the garden had heard the sound of a dog. It would have been possible, I was sure, to tie up and hide a dog in the bushes at the side of the house. Then the person would have been free to creep down to the summer house and murder Christopher. I thought of what Sarah had said about Christopher being asleep, his face in the pillow. Had he never known? Had the person who killed him not even looked at his face?

On the floor, at my feet, sat the red journal. *Red herring*, I thought. Taking me off down the wrong road. How could I have known, though, without finding out? I shrugged my shoulders. One door had closed. Now it was the door to *Cherry Tree Villa* that had to open.

It was clutching at straws. Why would the man who lives across the road, while walking his dog, slip into the summer house and murder Christopher Dean?

One of the things that Tony had taught me was that Murder means Motive. Random acts of violence were rare. Somebody was usually killed because some other person wanted them dead, hated them for some reason, or stood to gain in some way by their death.

I had thought, for a while, that Sarah and Jamie had a good reason to murder Christopher. But that had been wrong. They had been keeping his secret to protect him, not themselves.

What reason could the man across the road have for killing him? I didn't know. It was the most fragile of leads but it was all I had left. In the excitement of finding the journal I had almost forgotten about Billy Rogers, trapped, locked in a prison cell for something he hadn't done. Now that the mystery of the journal had been cleared up I began to see his face again, remember the bitter tone in his voice. I wondered whether he would ring me again. And if he did what on earth was I going to say to him?

"What are you going to say to him?" Brian said, seeming to give voice to my thoughts. He was nodding his head in the direction of *Cherry Tree Villa*.

"I'm not sure. Something about the dog?"

"The dog. OK." He was quiet for a few moments. "Give me one of your notepads. Didn't you say you had a tape recorder and a camera? Get them out as well. Let me do the talking. You look around."

The door opened almost as soon as we knocked on it. A grey-haired woman stood in front of us. She was casually dressed in a tracksuit made out of a velvet-like fabric. Around her neck were several gold chains and in her ears were two gold rings that looked like bangles.

"Yes?" she said, breathlessly.

"We're here to talk about the red setter? I believe my editor rang you earlier?" Brian said, raising his voice at the end of each sentence. He was holding the tiny tape recorder up in mid-air. "You won't mind if I record the conversation?"

"Dizzy? What do you want to know about Dizzy for?"

"Dizzy. That's right. That's not her show name, though, is it?"

"No, my dear, that's Ste. Marie du Jardin." The woman said, looking pleased with herself.

"Ste. Marie du Jardin, write that down, Patsy. Is Dizzy in? We'd love a photograph." Brian was looking and sounding every inch a newspaper reporter. I was impressed.

"What's this all about?" the woman said. "Only the dog belongs to my son and he's out at the moment."

"I'm sorry. I should have introduced myself. I'm Brian Kelly and this is Patsy Martin. We're reporters from the *Hampstead Advertiser*. We're doing a column about local pedigrees. A different one each week. Last week's was about the Afghan, you probably saw it?"

"A column in the newspaper." The woman began to smile. Then she held her hand out. "Mrs Hall. My son Arthur will be back shortly. I'm sure he'd be delighted for you to take a picture of Dizzy. He adores that dog. We actually have lots of our own photographs. Would you like to see them?"

"Would we like to see them, Patsy?" Brian said and Mrs Hall walked into the house while we followed her. I stabbed Brian in the back with my finger several times and whispered, *"Don't overdo it!"*

The album of photographs was huge and I could hear Brian oohing and aahing at different shots. I looked briefly myself. Dizzy the red setter looking regal, her coat the colour of varnished wood, running across Hampstead Heath, posing beside Mrs Hall. There were photos of her with a variety of people, members of the family, I supposed. One young woman had hair almost the same colour, flame red. It was quite striking.

While they were talking I looked around. The kitchen was like something out of a display showroom, fitted cupboards everywhere, shining saucepans hanging from a rack suspended from the ceiling. Over to the right was an Aga built into a brick wall that looked like an old chimney.

The noise of a car door banging came from outside and then a dog barking excitedly.

"That'll be Arthur," Mrs Hall said, rubbing her hands together. "He'll be so pleased to see you. He doesn't get many visitors!"

"Does your son work?" I said, trying to get an idea of what he was like. He was obviously well off, that much was clear.

"He works at home, my dear. He'll tell you, no doubt."

I was wondering what Arthur would look like. Holding my breath almost, crossing my fingers that he might walk in *looking* like a murderer. Was there any possibility that it could have been a random event, a moment of madness? Opportunist, is what the police call it. Arthur Hall, deranged young man, stalking the streets of Hampstead, stumbling on Christopher Dean asleep in the summer house, picking up the nearest thing to hand and bludgeoning him.

It was about as likely as a heavy snowfall in the middle of the desert.

The dog came tearing in first, running in circles around the breakfast bar, jumping up, its tail wagging furiously, back out into the hall and then back into the kitchen. I kept looking at the door to catch my first glimpse of Arthur Hall but he took a long time after opening the front door to appear.

"Arthur, there's some reporters here," Mrs Hall called. She turned to us. "He'll be pleased to see you. He loves visitors. He doesn't get about as much as he used to."

I looked back to the door and Arthur Hall wheeled himself in, his dog bouncing around the wheelchair wildly.

"Hello," he said cheerfully, "what's happening here?"

"Mr Hall? We've come about the dog," Brian said and went on to tell the same story that he'd told Mrs Hall.

I looked with dismay at Arthur Hall's wheelchair. It wasn't him, it couldn't have been him who crept into the Dean's garden on the night that Chris was murdered. I honestly felt like giving up and going home.

Mrs Hall had left us on our own. Arthur Hall was chatting amiably on about Dizzy and her exploits and I was taking notes. The album of photos had been left open at the one of the girl with the dazzling red hair.

I remembered the night of the murder, sitting in my mum's car just before the commotion from the Dean's maid. A person in a hooded tracksuit had walked along with the dog. That person hadn't been Arthur Hall. Could it have been a woman? When there was a gap in the talk I said, "How do you manage to exercise Dizzy, with your disability?"

"Fine, it's not a problem. I drive, Dizzy gets in the back of the car and I usually take him down the Heath every morning. Evenings sometimes Mum does it or occasionally, if Mum's out, Pippa will help."

"Pippa?" I said.

"That's Pippa," he said pointing at the photo. "She's a friend, works in the pet shop, on the Broadway. She often comes round to visit and she's happy to exercise Dizzy. Just a twenty-minute walk round the streets. Dizzy's very well-behaved. Pippa always takes the pooper-scooper so that no mess is left on the pavement. I think that's very important. You could put it in the column."

I dutifully wrote it down. All the time the word Pippa was running about in my head. *Pippa, Pippa, Pippa.*

"Out of interest, did your mother walk the dog on the night that the boy across the road was murdered?" I said, my pencil poised in mid-air.

"Oh, no, me and Mum were out that evening. We only heard about it all when we came back. No, Pippa walked Dizzy that night."

"She has her own key? That's handy," I said.

"Yes, we don't know what we'd do without her." I caught a hint of pride or affection in the young man's voice. I wondered if he was involved with her.

I looked down at my pad to see that I'd written it over and over again. *Pippa, Pippa, Pippa.* She had walked the dog that night.

"I think this is definitely the best photo of Dizzy," I said, pointing to the one of Pippa with the dog. "Would it be possible for us to borrow it? We'd return it to you as soon as we made a copy."

"Of course," Arthur Hall said. "Pippa will be thrilled to have her picture in the paper."

I took the photo and picked up my pad. "Pippa's surname?" I said. "For the caption?"

"Adams. Pippa Adams," Arthur said proudly.

Pippa Adams, Pippa Adams. *Philippa Adams.* The daughter of Mrs Adams who was killed in a car crash. She had been walking the dog on the night of the murder.

"Do you have an address," I said, "just so that we can get permission from her? To use the photo?" I had my pencil poised in mid-air. Philippa Adams, whose mother was killed in a car crashed by Christopher Dean's father. It was a huge coincidence. It had to be significant.

"I can give you her address," Arthur Hall smiled, fondly, "but you won't find her there. She's gone off for a few days, to see friends, she said."

"When did she go?"

"Early Tuesday morning, I think. At least we didn't see her after Monday, you know, the night that poor boy was murdered. She's good like that. Even though she was going off on a holiday she still walked Dizzy for us. That's the sort of person she is. Thoughtful, caring. She probably hasn't even heard about that terrible business. She knew them, you know, the Deans. At least I think that's what she said."

"Right," I said, copying down her address anyway. On the bottom of the page I wrote the words, *thoughtful, caring*. And underlined them.

20
Stepsisters

In the car, on the way back to Walthamstow, I tried the obvious theory on Brian.

"Philippa Adams has some kind of grudge against the Dean family. Her mother was killed in the car crash. She has decided to get even in some way."

On my lap I had the photo I had kept from Sarah's shoe box, Philippa and Sarah together, dressed up, on the back the words, *Sarah and Philippa, Christmas*. I also remembered the other photos, the ones where Mrs Adams's face had been crossed out.

"But why kill Christopher? What has he got to do with it?"

"I don't know," I said. "Philippa Adams couldn't

have known that Christopher felt responsible. That didn't emerge for years. I need to talk to Sarah again. Maybe she can throw some light on the whole thing."

"I'll be working all afternoon. And there's football training tonight," Brian said, "and I'm meant to be helping out at the warehouse tomorrow…"

"Oh, listen, you've driven me round enough. I'm really grateful, Brian. I'll be fine. I'll ring Sarah Dean, talk to her over the phone. I need to spend a bit of time in the office anyway. I'll call you, if anything important comes up."

"Sure you won't forget?" Brian said.

"Positive. Hey, I'll call you even if nothing important comes up!"

I meant it. Brian dropped me off at the office and I watched him drive away towards the market. I liked him. I liked him a lot. He had been a godsend; good company, funny, warm and willing to go along with my suggestions about the case but not afraid to disagree with me if he thought I was wrong.

He'd been like Billy.

I let myself into the office, picked up the mail from the floor and sat down at my desk. My mood evaporated as I imagined Billy, locked in a prison cell, a bucket in the corner to use for a toilet. Why had he gone out to that summer house, picked up that lampstand? Why hadn't he just stayed in the kitchen?

Because he'd heard what he'd thought was a cry for help, a moaning sound that turned out to be a dog. He'd gone out into that garden to *help* someone and now he was locked away.

The word *injustice* sat stubbornly in my head. There was also a feeling of panic, somewhere deep down in my chest. Was I going to be able to find the murderer? Or was Billy going to spend years of his life in prison for something he hadn't done?

I had a lead. Philippa Adams was in the area at the time of the murder. Had she some grudge against the Deans? I reached over to the phone and was about to dial Sarah's number when I noticed the answer-phone button blinking on and off. I pressed the button and heard Sarah Dean's voice.

"Pat, I won't be around for a few days, maybe until Thursday. I'm taking Jamie off to stay with a friend for a while. He needs the break and, to be honest, so do I. We've been to the police. They were pretty interested in the stuff we told them. They're going to release Chris's body later this week so I'll be arranging the funeral when I get back. I'll call you Thursday."

A feeling of irritation itched at me. Sarah Dean had gone away and wasn't coming back until Thursday. I wouldn't be able to ask her about Philippa Adams until then. I loitered around the office for a while tidying papers that didn't need tidying. Then I decided to go home.

I could hear the shower from upstairs as I opened

the front door. The radio was on as well, playing pop songs, the kind my mum usually turned off. I wondered how she was. In the middle of the whole mess I had quite forgotten about her depression.

In the living room I sat down on the sofa and laid all my stuff out on the coffee table. In the corner of my eye I could see the briefcase sitting, looking aloof, oblivious of the files and bits of paper that my mum had stuffed into it since the previous evening.

She had been very angry at me for taking it. I'd tried to explain but she'd been preoccupied and distant, tipping out my stuff and rigorously filling each compartment with papers and files. *I'm really sorry*, I'd kept saying, keen to get off and read Christopher Dean's journal.

Sorry's not enough sometimes! Not enough! she'd shouted before going up to bed. I'd had the feeling that her anger and her words hadn't really been intended for me. Another time I'd have gone and tried to comfort her. I hadn't, though. I'd had too much to do on the case.

I listened for a moment to the shower going off. Then I heard my mum's voice, *singing*. I raised my eyebrows and started to sort through my things.

I looked again at the photo of Philippa Adams with Sarah, dating back many years, two little girls dressed up for a Christmas party. Then I looked at the adult. A striking girl, a mop of red hair framing her face, her smile wide. I narrowed my eyes to look more closely at the top of her forehead. A blemish of some sort, a line, almost unnoticeable. I took the picture over to the window and saw it more clearly. A faint scar. A couple of inches long, just under the hairline. Otherwise her skin was clear.

Had the scar come from the crash, when she had lost her mother? Had Philippa felt bitter about that? It was all so long ago, though. Could it have any bearing on Christopher's death?

I imagined Philippa creeping through the trees and bushes of the Dean's garden. She would have tied the red setter up somewhere, in the bushes perhaps. She had slipped into the summer house, ready for what? Murder? But Christopher had been killed by a blow from the lampstand. If someone had decided in advance to murder, wouldn't they have brought their own weapon? What exactly had Philippa gone in there for?

Although I had no real evidence for it I pictured her slipping into the summer house. Christopher would have been there, asleep on the sofa. What was it that Sarah Dean had said? He had been face down on the sofa, she hadn't seen his *face*. Philippa must have looked at him there, his blond hair loose, not unlike his sister's, lying asleep on the sofa. Had she planned to kill him? Thought there might be a weapon of some sort there? Perhaps she had been in that summer house on other evenings, checking it out. But why?

Why would she want to kill Chris? She was much more likely to have had feelings towards Sarah Dean. *Sarah* had come out of the accident unscathed.

I heard my mum coming down the stairs, her footsteps quick, light.

"Oh, Patsy," she said, cheerfully. "This came for you, after you left this morning."

She handed me a brown envelope with my name typed neatly on the front. I put it down on the table, my mind still concentrating on the photos of Philippa Adams.

Could Philippa have had a grudge against Sarah Dean? Not Christopher at all?

Sarah Dean had disliked Philippa's mother. There were the crosses on the photos in her shoe box. Was there general animosity between them? Rows, disagreements? Could Sarah have been jealous of her father's new girlfriend? Was it the case that Philippa, knowing of this, had some sort of hatred for Sarah? That when she walked into that summer house and saw someone lying face down on the settee, the blond hair long and loose, she actually thought that it was *Sarah Dean* lying there.

In spite of myself I began to feel excited by this thought. Philippa had not meant to kill Christopher Dean at all. She had picked up the lamp and hit out at the person she had thought was Sarah!

Could it have been as simple as that? I picked up

the brown envelope and began to open it. Maybe Sarah had made things difficult for Mrs Adams, unpleasant for Philippa. I remembered the photos with the crosses; as if Sarah had physically crossed Mrs Adams out of her dad's life.

And then, after the accident, Sarah still had her brother. Philippa had no one.

I pulled open the brown envelope that my mum had given me. Inside was a photocopied letter and a small card that said PRISON PASS. I scanned the letter. It was from the remand centre that Billy had been sent to. It was a visitor's pass. It meant that I could go and see him. I looked at the address at the top of the letter. The place was in Kent. It was definitely possible to travel there and back in a day. I allowed a gathering excitement to bubble through and punched at the air with my fist.

I could go and see Billy!

"Do you want some tea?" My mum's voice interrupted my thoughts. I noticed that her face was made-up and her hair newly washed. She looked nicer than she had for weeks.

"No thanks," I said. I was thinking about the visit and whether I had enough money for the train ticket. I stood up, not sure of what to do. A knock at my front door jolted me out of my thoughts.

"I'll get it!" I could hear my mum's voice, bright, vibrant. The door opened and I could hear her mumbling and another voice.

"Look who's here," she said, coming into the living room. Behind her was Gerry, the boyfriend who had dumped her some weeks before. He had a silly smile on his face, his small round glasses glinting at me.

"Hello, Pats," he said, and stood with his hands in the pockets of his denim jacket.

She had taken him back! I couldn't believe it!

"Mum?" I said but she just stood smiling foolishly, one hand on Gerry's shoulder.

I said no more. I swept all my stuff up into my old rucksack, went upstairs and closed my bedroom door. I was not going to sit around and listen to the Two-Timer and my mum canoodling together.

21
Prison

Billy looked awful.

His skin was yellow and his clothes looked as if they hadn't been changed for days. It wasn't like him. He was usually so particular about hygiene.

"Billy!" I said, with as much affection in my voice as I could muster. I reached out and grabbed his hand. He didn't respond in the same way, though. He didn't hold my hand back, he simply let me hold his.

"Patsy." He smiled weakly.

The visitors' room was painted a dull yellow. It was long and low, the ceiling seemed to be touching my head. Around the edge the guards stood talking together, like teachers on playground duty. I half expected to see them drinking steaming cups of coffee and pulling out a whistle in case of trouble.

"Are you eating all right?" I said. "I've brought you some fruit."

He nodded. I felt like I was a hospital visitor. On the table between us was a bag of fat grapes and a bunch of bananas that looked like a disembodied hand. I gave a little smile and pulled my hat further down over my forehead. Then I took it off.

"Relax, Patsy," he said, and leaned back on the chair.

From behind him I heard a guffaw and the words, "*All right, Bill?*" I looked across to see a youth with an almost completely bald head. He had wide shoulders and a thick middle. He didn't look fat though, he looked solid, muscular. He was grinning widely at me and Billy, and I saw that two of his front teeth had gold caps on them.

I didn't like the look of him. I knew it was narrow-minded and prejudiced but I couldn't help it. I looked away, trying to ignore the suggestive leer he was giving me and Billy. I found myself staring at a sign that said *Prisoners should refrain from necking.* It was one of those old-fashioned words, like something my uncle Tony would use. It meant kissing and cuddling. Fat chance of any of that, I thought.

"So, are you sharing?" I said, keeping my voice light.

"Yes, a kid from Greenwich. Not a bad bloke."

"What's he done?" I said, looking warily around the room, my eye avoiding direct contact with anyone.

"He hasn't *done* anything, Patsy. He's been accused of mugging. He says he's innocent. That's it in here, see. We're all innocent."

"A mugger," I said, picturing Billy sharing a cell with a callous, unpleasant character.

"That's him," Billy said, nodding his head to one side.

I looked around. A kid with carrot-coloured hair, who looked about sixteen was sitting, crying his eyes out to an older woman across a table. She had her hand on his head, stroking him. Now and then she looked warily over at us. I realized then that the boy had probably told her he was sharing with a *murderer*. She looked visibly shocked.

"Have you seen Sarah?" Billy said.

"Yes."

"Does she still think I did it?"

"I don't know," I said honestly. "A lot's happened since I spoke to you on the phone."

I proceeded to tell him. We spent a long time going over the business with Christopher and Jamie that had led to Christopher running out and driving into Billy's parents. He was incredulous when I told him about the spiders, almost laughing out loud. He calmed down, though, when I described Jamie Kent, locked in the dark.

"I know what it's like to be locked up," he said

quietly. I noticed that for most of the time we were talking he'd been tapping the side of his hand gently but purposefully on the table.

"No wonder Christopher Dean had such bad dreams," I said, finishing off. I planned next to tell him about Philippa Adams and the lead that I had there. He interrupted me, though.

"What a nasty piece of work he was. Bullied and frightened this other lad and then went out and killed my mum and dad. If anyone deserved to die, then he did."

"Billy!" I said in a loud whisper. I looked around and caught the eye of one of the security guards.

"Listen, Pat. I've been in here a week and I've heard some stories that would make your hair stand on end."

"But nevertheless…"

"There are some people who just don't deserve any sympathy and he was one of them."

"But he didn't deserve to die."

For some reason it was important for me to hear Billy say it, to see the old Billy again, the one who didn't throw litter on the pavement and who never parked on double yellow lines.

"Sometimes, when I was in that house, waiting for Sarah, I'd hear him humming a tune. Humming a tune! My mum and dad are dead because of him and he's humming a tune! You know I felt my temper rising…"

"He paid a price …" I said. The conversation was not going the way I wanted it to at all.

"Not a big enough price…" he cut across me.

"Temper? What do you mean?" I interrupted. "You haven't got a temper."

"Patsy, you don't know everything about me."

I sat in silence for a moment, still holding on to his hand even though it felt cold, clammy, like a child being taken on a walk that it didn't want to go on.

"Billy," I said, "this isn't like you."

"Maybe I've changed. Christopher Dean was a rich kid who managed to smash my family to bits. Maybe that made me sick to my stomach and I changed."

"He did change, Billy. He was ashamed of what he'd done…"

"A lot of good it's done me."

"Anyway…" I said, determined to move the conversation on, "the night of the murder. You said you heard a dog. Well, by coincidence…"

"I don't know. Maybe I heard a dog, maybe I didn't. I don't know any more."

He stood up, wearily pulling his hand away from mine. The skinhead from across the room gave him a wave with a lit cigarette.

"The longer I'm in here, the more time I spend on my own, in that cell, the more I think that Christopher Dean deserved what he got."

And he turned and walked away. Without a goodbye, without a wave.

On the table in front of me sat the untouched grapes and the bananas.

On the train station I sat and cried. I let the tears come out, I almost willed them to come out, one after the other, wetting my skin. I put my hands up to my eyes and rubbed them dry, only to find my fingers black with mascara. I let a train go by while I washed myself in the station toilet. I stood, leaning against the wall and let the hand drier blow up at my face, my hair billowing out behind me.

What had happened to Billy? In just eight days he had become hard, intractable.

I hadn't even been able to tell him about Philippa Adams and her possible grudge against Sarah Dean. That was the one bit of good news I had, a tiny pin-prick of light in the darkness and he hadn't been interested.

All sorts of strange forebodings were working away inside me. In a case filled with uncertainties there had always been one solid thing that I had had: the knowledge that Billy Rogers was innocent.

I remembered his words: *He deserved what he got. Christopher Dean deserved what he got.*

At that moment, waiting for that train, I just wasn't sure any more. Of anything.

When I got off the train in central London I

didn't want to go home. I knew my mum would be there with the Two-Timer, Gerry. Instead I went to see a film and then walked aimlessly around Covent Garden, looking in shops and watching the buskers performing for the tourists.

Sarah Dean was coming back the next day. I would speak to her about Philippa Adams then. After that I would know what to do.

The next morning I got up early. I had no idea what time Sarah Dean would be back. I decided to go into the office, do some work, and then, mid-morning, close up and go up to Hampstead. Even if Sarah hadn't got back by then there was always Josie to talk to, as well as Megan the maid.

While I was at the office the postman brought up a registered letter. I signed for it, thinking it was some legal papers for my uncle.

It was addressed to me, though, marked for my attention but sent to the office. I was puzzled. I opened it and saw some papers, photocopied, attached to a covering letter. The heading was printed, HM Prison, Sheldon House. Handwritten, across the page, were the words, *Found these after all, hope they help to give a picture of how mixed-up Chris Dean was. David Geraghy.*

It was the report from Christopher Dean's school, St Edward's. I glanced over it. It referred to the incident of bullying which had brought his asthma on three years before. I was tempted to throw it aside, bury it with all the stuff in the red journal as being irrelevant. I didn't, though.

William Nash was the pupil concerned ... mistreated over a number of weeks ... strong suggestions from the boys that Dean was the bully ... No real evidence for this ... William Nash severely traumatized by events not yet clearly explained ... boy is under medical supervision and won't be returning to St Edward's ... Dean denied any involvement and rigorous questioning precipitated several asthma attacks which meant he had to be sent home on medical grounds...

I sat back with my mouth open. It all fitted. Christopher hadn't been the victim of the bullying at school, he had been the bully. I opened the red journal and took out the school photo that had been there. A section of a class photograph. Chris and two boys either side of him. Behind him a couple of others. Had one of those boys been the one who he had traumatized? I didn't know.

I put the photo down and picked up the one of Philippa Adams posing beside Dizzy the dog. Had I nearly solved the mystery? Was it that Philippa had wanted to kill Sarah and had killed Christopher by mistake? Then gone on holiday? Perhaps she hadn't even known she'd made the mistake until the next day when it had come out in the papers. How had she felt? Sorry? Annoyed with herself? More determined than before?

An uneasiness made me sit up. Was there a possibility that Philippa Adams might want to finish the job she had started? To kill Sarah Dean?

I tried to keep calm as I locked up the office. It was just like me to dramatize the situation. I had absolutely no proof. I could be completely wrong, I knew that. It was just a theory, none of it was fact.

I found myself walking quickly, though, bumping into people on the pavement. I couldn't help but push against the crowd at the train station, leaping into the carriage at the last minute.

I was first off at Gospel Oak station and half ran, half walked up the hill towards High Heath.

22
Accidental Death

There was no answer at Sarah Dean's house, even though her car was parked outside. There was no Megan or Josie, either. In the mood I was in, it was all distinctly ominous. I hung around for a couple of minutes, stabbing at the bell with my finger, then I decided to walk round to the back.

I went slowly by the willow and around by the thick bushes that I was sure Philippa Adams had crept through on the night of the murder. In and out, quickly, silently, perhaps even before Jamie Kent had got there. The dog had been tied up somewhere, maybe further down the garden. As I went by, I peered in each of the windows to see if there was any sign of anyone. Each room I passed was empty though and as I went on I was beginning to wonder whether I'd made a wasted journey; Sarah not having arrived back and Megan and Josie out shopping somewhere.

When I got round the back the French doors were wide open.

"Sarah?" I said, quietly, and walked towards them. I stopped and looked round the garden, down towards the summer house. It was empty, the police tape gone, the trees and bushes staring back at me, giving nothing away. An uneasy feeling began to niggle away inside me. Where was everyone?

I stood back for a moment, to the side of the door, looking down the garden where only ten days before Christopher had been killed. Megan must have come out of the kitchen door that night, started walking towards the summer house, perhaps half-way down she had broken into a run. Had she known something was wrong? Or had she simply been looking for Billy or Christopher?

And then, on the white mosaic floor, the blood, post-box red, in a puddle beside his head.

Had Megan started to scream then? Or had the sound stuck in her throat while she stood and looked at Billy, kneeling over the body, the lampstand still in his hand, the broken green bulb strewn across the floor like leaves blown in from the garden.

Had Billy killed Christopher?

For the first time I asked myself the question seriously.

A noise from somewhere inside the house broke into my thoughts. I stepped inside, pushing Billy out of my mind. To my left was the kitchen, the table set with three plates. Some cold meat and salad sat on them and beside each was a tiny roll that had been split and partially buttered. There were some flies lazily buzzing around the plates and a wasp had dropped into a glass of juice. One of the chairs had been tipped up and was lying on its back on the floor.

A meal had been interrupted. Someone had come in, perhaps through the French doors as I was doing. Sarah, Josie and Megan had stopped eating, put their knives and forks down on the table beside their unfinished bread and drinks.

Holding my breath I walked across to the side where a teapot sat. I put my hands around it; it was still lukewarm. How long ago had it happened? Minutes? Longer?

I looked at the chair on the floor. Had one of them resisted?

Was it Philippa Adams? She had tried to kill Sarah and ended up killing her brother instead. Is that why she was there now? To get the right person?

I knew I had to call the police. That was clear. I was about to pick up the phone when I saw the newspaper cutting on the floor. I bent down to retrieve it. It was small, just a scrap of paper.

The headline read, JUGGERNAUT KILLS SIXTEEN-YEAR-OLD. I read over the article, glancing anxiously around the room from time to time. *Billy Nash, an unemployed youth of Norwood, West London, was killed instantly yesterday in a tragic road accident. He was hit in broad daylight by a fifteen-ton lorry. Local residents say that they had warned the authorities about the appalling increase of traffic on city streets...* That was all it said. The date was clear though. Almost exactly a year before.

I was interrupted by sounds that seemed to come from below. A muffled voice, another. I stood absolutely still and listened as hard as I could. *Billy Nash.* The name rang a bell.

Then I heard the voices distinctly, from below. I looked down at the floor. Philippa Adams had taken them to the basement, I was sure. I held on to the strange newspaper cutting, wondering what I should do. I looked at the phone again. How long would it take the police to arrive? Maybe it would take them too long. For a moment I couldn't move, indecision rooted me to the spot.

In the end I pulled myself along the hallway towards the basement door, taking care that my steps were silent. The door was ajar and I pushed it gently open. The stairs down to the basement were in darkness but the light from the long playroom shone brightly and I could hear the whir of the air conditioner. I crept down the first couple of stairs.

The sound of a strong female voice came from the far end of the room and as I descended further, centimetre by centimetre, I could see a woman's back, just one woman. She seemed to be talking all the time, more to herself than anything else.

I was puzzled slightly by what I saw. Instead of three women being held by a red-haired woman, there was just one woman, her hair a mousy brown, her back to me talking on and on about "Poor dear Billy", who deserved better, who had never hurt a fly. For a brief moment I thought she was talking about Billy Rogers, my Billy.

I was wrong, though. As I stood, holding my breath, I recognized her voice. It was Megan, the housemaid.

Megan. The maid. Who had discovered Christopher's body. I didn't understand. Where was Philippa Adams, who had a grudge against Sarah Dean?

She turned round then and faced me. In her hand was a long knife, its blade glinting under the bright playroom lights.

"The detective!" she said. "You've finally worked it out?"

I didn't say anything. I hadn't worked anything out. From behind her I could see the key to the sauna still in its lock. There was no sign of Sarah or Josie.

Megan looked at my hand which still held the newspaper report.

"You've seen what happened to my brother?" I heard her voice but I was looking at the knife which seemed to have grown bigger since I stood there. Behind her the sauna sat like an innocent garden shed. Through the glass window I could see that it was pitch dark. Had she locked Sarah and Josie in there?

"What happened to him, your brother?" I said.

"He killed him. Christopher Dean *killed* my brother. Do you hear that in there!" she screamed out suddenly, her voice aimed like a missile towards the sauna. No sound came back and I got this horrible clammy feeling. Surely she hadn't done anything to them?

"What do you mean?" I said, keeping my voice as calm as possible.

"He was a nasty character. He enjoyed making fun of people, making them unhappy. My brother was only sixteen. *Sixteen!* Do you hear?" She directed her words again to the sauna.

I looked around me. The covered snooker table was a few feet away and from the corner of my eye I saw the snooker cues lying on top of the sheeting. She looked back then, still talking.

"He was just a kid in school. Someone that Christopher Dean saw as weak. Someone that he could pick on! He didn't tell a soul... Not until it was too late."

She was moving her hand up and down and I saw

the knife glint, the light from the ceiling flash on to it. There was still no sound from the sauna. Had she hurt them? Were they in need of medical help? I looked to the side again and saw the snooker cue, lying invitingly, only a step away.

"He had a nervous breakdown, see? Dropped out of school. Oh, it was long after Dean had gone to prison. But he was never the same, never the same. He was quiet and frightened of his own shadow. That's what Christopher Dean did to my brother!"

"Christopher was an unstable young man. We know that, Megan..." I said, inching myself sideways.

"He tried to get a job, a college place, but he couldn't hold them down. He was distracted. He never got over the bad time he'd had with Dean. One day he walked out of the house and never came back. My mother was completely devastated."

"Chris was psychologically unstable, Megan." I managed to move another few inches.

"We got a visit from the police. He'd been living on the streets, see! On the streets! My brother, among the filth and the cold and loneliness. And one day he was crossing the road and he didn't look. That's what the policeman said, he didn't look. The lorry hit him and killed him outright. Accidental Death they said, *Accidental Death*. But it wasn't an accident. My brother was murdered by Dean."

Her voice was getting higher and I noticed that

she had started to rub her fingers up and down the knife. I couldn't help it, I glanced over at the snooker cue and then back to her. She saw my look and her forehead crinkled. She opened her mouth to speak when there was a sudden pounding sound from behind her, from inside the sauna. She turned with surprise and I knew it was then or never. I reached for the snooker cue and swung it around, closing my eyes when it hit her heavily on the shoulder, my stomach collapsing with the fright of actually *striking* someone.

She fell forward and the knife dropped out of her hand. I kicked my foot out and propelled it off down the room, spinning on the floor like a top, coming to a stop at the other end near the stacks of toys boxed up, and labelled with Lego or Playmobile.

I was standing above her with the cue in both my hands. I must have looked serious because every time I breathed heavily or moved she flinched with her eyes as though she thought I was going to hit her.

"Open the door!" I said in a commanding voice. "Open it!" I felt as if I had a rifle in my hand, not a long thin stick.

She struggled up and turned the key. The door opened on to the black interior, like a cave, and I remembered the spiders that had been left there, the boy, Jamie Kent, who had felt like he'd been buried there.

Sarah Dean came out first, her eyes squinting at the light. Josie followed her, holding on to the younger woman's arm, her back bent, her face ashen.

"Are you all right?" I said, still holding the snooker cue, like a sword pointed at Megan.

Sarah went across to her. "Megan, I know he was bad but he was sick. He blanked it all out. He hated that side of himself." She was still defending her brother.

But Megan just pushed her head into her hands and said nothing.

"Call the police, Sarah," I said. "Call them now."

My arms were trembling with a mixture of fright and tension. I knew then that I would never be able to swing that cue back and hit out again with it. If Megan wanted she could just walk out of the cellar and disappear into the streets around. I wouldn't have been able to stop her.

She didn't seem to want to, though. I let the stick drop and stood, like a solitary guard, while she sat on the floor and cried. In the back of my head I could hear Sarah's footsteps as she went up the stairs of the basement and out to the phone.

23
Brothers and Sisters

"William Nash was her brother. She loved him. She hated what Christopher Dean had done to him."

Brian was sitting beside me on my sofa. He had his arm around my shoulder and I was lying against him. It was getting dark, the room was in shades of grey but we hadn't put the light on.

"So she bore a grudge for all that time, got a job with the Deans and planned to do away with him."

"I'm not sure it was ever as calculated as that. I suppose we'll have to wait until the trial. I wonder if she just hated him, watched him, living in luxury after having been the cause of so much unhappiness. Don't forget Billy's parents as well. Christopher had ended their lives and there he was, out of prison in only three years."

"But why did she hold a knife to Sarah Dean and the housekeeper?"

"I don't know what made her snap. Sarah said they were eating lunch, just chatting. She said she started discussing Christopher's funeral arrangements with Josie and Megan kept butting in, referring to her own brother's funeral. She brought out the newspaper report and in the end threw her chair back and let it all out. Sarah said that once she started talking she seemed to lose control, picking up the knife from the worktop."

"And Philippa Adams?" Brian said, after a few minutes of quiet.

"It turned out that Sarah knew she was working locally. Sarah said there never was bad feeling between her and Mrs Adams. Or Philippa, come to that. She said Philippa phoned her up on the morning after Christopher was murdered. Said how sorry she was about it. She'd been rushing off, you see, to get a train. She'd just put Dizzy back into Mr Hall's house and ignored the commotion, thinking it was just a row of some sort."

"What about the crosses on the photographs, over Mrs Adams's face?"

"Sarah wasn't clear about that, didn't want to talk about it. I think she's still protecting Christopher. It seems the sort of thing that he might have done. He didn't like sharing his sister with Jamie Kent. Maybe he didn't like sharing his dad with Mrs Adams."

We sat quietly for a minute, the room almost completely dark. I knew, in a moment or so, I would have to get up and turn the lights on. It was comfortable being there with Brian, alone in the house, his voice breaking the silence from time to time. After the tension of the previous few hours, the confusion, the questions from the police, the sight of Megan Nash being taken away, staring mournfully from the back seat of a patrol car, I needed some space, someone to talk to.

My mum had been out so I'd called Brian and he had come and picked me up from Hampstead Police Station. Sarah Dean had hugged me, her thin arms around my back, her long hair blowing across my face.

As we drove off she'd stood on the steps of the police station, a lonely figure. I'd wondered what would happen to her. She was a rich woman, or so her mother said. Would Billy contact her again, once he was released?

As we'd passed the end of her road I'd thought about Christopher Dean, coming out of prison, looking for his memory, blithely unaware of the malicious person he had been. The memory journal had been a key to a past that he should never have known about.

"What about the animal sounds, the dog whining in the dark? Where did that come from?"

"Next door," I said. "Next-door's dog had had

pups some days before. Nobody knew. They're very private around that part of Hampstead."

I'd got that wrong, like a lot of other things. It was one of the frustrations of working alone, without the co-operation of the police. Obvious questions were left unanswered and could grow into seemingly significant clues that turned out to point in the wrong direction.

It turned out all right in the end, though. This time.

"When is Billy Rogers being released?"

"Tomorrow morning. There'll be a special hearing in front of a judge. It's just a formality really. I'll get my mum to come and meet him."

"You don't want me to come then?"

"No," I said. After seeing Billy in prison I had no idea what he would be like. The old Billy? Easygoing? Pleasant? Or would he be embittered, callous, like he had seemed the other night? Either way I was not sure how he would react to me being with Brian Martin.

A scraping sound broke into my thoughts and I heard the front door open.

"It's my mum!" I hissed. I stood up and clicked the table lamp on just as she walked into the living room. Gerry, the Two-Timer, was with her.

"Why was it so dark in here?"

"I was just resting my eyes," I said hopelessly. Gerry's face had broken into a grin and they were both looking at Brian.

"This is my friend, Brian," I said to both of them, averting my eyes like a teenager who had been caught having a first kiss.

"There were two phone messages for you, Patsy," my mum said, in a businesslike manner. "One was from that awful police person, Heather Warren. She says she's back from her holidays and what was it you wanted her for? Honestly, that woman always speaks as though she's giving orders."

My eye caught Gerry the Two-Timer's for a moment but I looked quickly away.

"The other message was from Tony. He and Geraldine came back early. Apparently the rain was too much for him. I could've told him. He wanted to know whether everything was all right. Naturally I told him about Billy Rogers. He was shocked. He's coming round to see what he can do. He's got good contacts, you know."

That was typical of Tony. *He* had contacts. *He* would be able to help. He wanted centre stage as usual.

And yet, there he was, dropping everything to see if he could help. That was typical of him as well.

"I don't think I'll be needing him this time," I said. "I think it's all been sorted out."

I said good night to Brian on my doorstep.

It was a long kiss and then he stood back, looking unsure.

"What worries me," he said, "is that when Billy Rogers come home you won't want to see me again."

"No." I said it immediately. I was sure that wouldn't happen.

"OK, then. Maybe you'll go off to university and meet some intellectual types. Someone who wouldn't know a football from a boiled egg."

"No, of course not!" I said without hesitation.

University. It was only a week or so away and it was like another world.

"See you then, Miss Detective. Look after yourself." He held his fingers up at me, in the shape of a gun. Then he made a popping sound with his mouth, blew imaginary smoke from the end of the barrel and walked off.

I smiled stupidly.

My uncle Tony was in the kitchen with my mum. I'd filled him in on everything that had happened. His face was impassive, nodding slightly now and then. His moustache was fuller and more solid-looking. He had a white T-shirt on and a number of gold chains hanging around his neck that I hadn't seen before. He had the look of a Mafia man. I wondered if my aunt Geraldine liked it.

He was going to go soon, back home, and I was trying to build up enough confidence to tell him something. My mum would have to know as well.

It was about the choice between going to university and becoming a proper private detective. It was about burying myself in books for three years or working, as a kind of apprentice with my uncle, learning the job, like a trade, so that I could become professional at it.

That was the choice I had to make. Providing he would let me.

I decided to count to ten inside my head and then go out to the kitchen and tell them. I started slowly so that I could build up my courage. One ... two ... three ... four ... five...